THIS ONE'S A REAL
MOTHERFUCKER, FIVE...

"... dazzling art and an interesting psychological drama"

– Bloody-Disgusting.com

"This comic is a really great read, like the kind of stuff we used to get from *Preacher, Y: The Last Man,* and *Transmetropolitan.*"

– IGN.com

"Kowalski's art continues to impress, using light and shadow as his weapons, just as much as the understated colour spectrum that has become a signature of the series so far. *Sex* is a slow-builder, and one that we suspect will ultimately reward a reader with stamina and longevity."

– Behind the Panels

"... the art, the color, the textures, or the writing, everything about this comic is good and when it all comes together it is something amazing."

– Speak Geeky To Me

"... a great read with great characters who are all a bit off and deeply complex. 5/5 stars."

– Unleash the Fanboy

"Do yourselves a favor and just give it a chance, better yet, read it with your significant other. Do it. Come on. You know you want to."

– Ket's Comics

"... under the radar but sure to be a classic"

– Geeked Out Nation

"Joe Casey and Piotr Kowalski have created a stylish look at an often overlooked part of the superhero genre."

– Comic Book Resources

".. the long-sought-after 'HBO of Superheroes' – a long term, adult oriented story that tries to say something not just about the genre but about society."

– Sequart Organization

"... another sharp, twisted take on superhero clichés."

– Publishers Weekly

"... taps into an area that is rarely given light in the comic world."

– Comic Bastards

"*Sex* continues to keep you guessing at what it's got up it's sleeve next... worth the tension and anticipation."

– Unleash the Fanboy

"... the maturity extends to Piotr Kowalski's art, which is incredible for an artist of his relative level of experience in comics."

– Multiversity Comics

"As creators, what Kowalski, Casey and Simpson love is pillow talk, which is perfect for a comic called *Sex.*"

– Comics Bulletin

"Joe Casey has done a lot of thoughtful and provocative work in the comics industry but *Sex* is probably one of his finest yet."

— All-Comic

"... gorgeous artwork from Kowalski, who ensures that the reader inhabits the sticky work of Saturn City."

— Behind the Panels

"... anyone who approaches *Sex* with an open mind and a willingness to take their time with it is much more likely to have a fulfilling experience than those who try to rush it."

— Comic Bastards

"... if you miss the honed sense of danger you got when reading *The Dark Knight Returns*, *Watchmen* and *American Flagg*! it might be time for you to check out the Image comic, *Sex*."

— Comics Alliance

"*Sex* pulls off a great feat by embracing familiar elements from past famous works while feeling wholly unique."

— IGN.com

"... an adult comic in the truest sense in that it wants to approach the subject of sex in an actually adult manner, which is very rare to find in comics."

— Front Towards Gamer

"The genius of *Sex* is how those subplots continue to evolve and morph into more story without reaching a 'conclusion' because that's not what this book, or storytelling in a general sense, is about."

— Nothing But Comics

"... provides the graphic nudity that its title suggests, but also keenly takes on the interactions among big business, the media, political power players, gang bosses and former superheroes and villains."

— Big Glasgow Comic Page

"... it will leave you wanting more, another itch you can't wait to scratch."

— Nerdlocker.com

"*Sex* is extremely interesting and quite dynamic."

— Rhymes With Geek

"Casey has written a vast and layered tale that has been as entertaining as it has been dirty."

— Comic Bastards

"... a labor of love that is overflowing with pathos, humor, and humanity."

— Multiversity Comics

"... showcases Saturn City as a living breathing entity full of many moving parts and players."

— Comics Bulletin

BOOK FIVE:

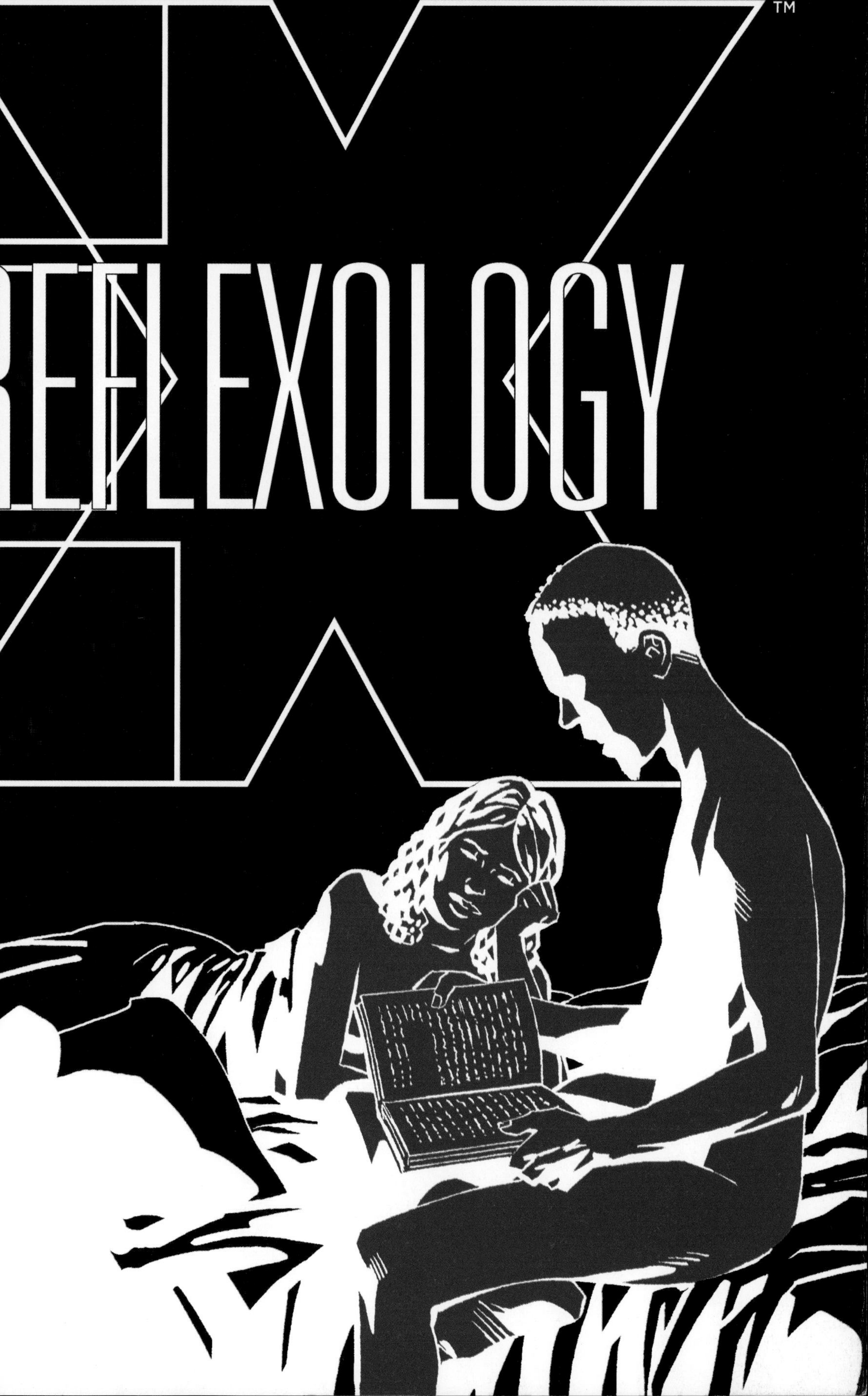
REFLEXOLOGY
TM

www.manofaction.tv

SEX Book Five: Reflexology
First printing. February 2017.

ISBN: 978-1-63215-904-5

Published by Image Comics, Inc.

Office of publication:
2701 NW Vaughn St., Suite 780,
Portland, OR 97210.

For international licensing inquiries, write to:
foreignlicensing@imagecomics.com

Printed in the USA. For information regarding the CPSIA on this printed material call: 203-595-3636 and provide reference #RICH–721828.

JOE CASEY WRITER
PIOTR KOWALSKI ARTIST
BRAD SIMPSON COLORIST
RUS WOOTON LETTERER
SONIA HARRIS GRAPHIC DESIGNER

WHO IS IN SEX?

SIMON COOKE
Rich. Retired. Repressed.

ANNABELLE LAGRAVENESE
Club owner. Catty. Confident.

KEENAN WADE
Courageous. Undaunted. Infiltrator.

QUINN
lentor. Puppet master.
eceased.

WARREN AZOFF
Lawyer. Confidant. Pimpmeister.

JULIETTE JEMAS
Journalist. Single. Single-minded.

MASAI
Break. Boss. Bad ass.

LORRAINE BAINES
Larry". Cooke Company
xecutive. Capable.

THE ALPHA BROS.
Cha Cha & Dolph. Criminal. Ambiguous.

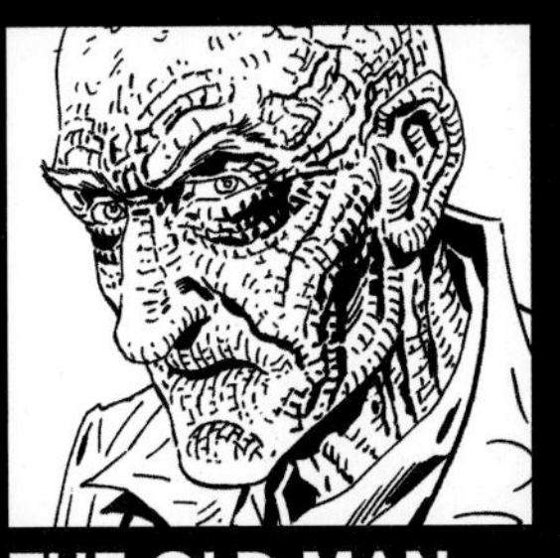

THE OLD MAN
Gangster. Weary. Deceased.

ELLIOT K. BARNES
Loyal employee. Awkward. Unhinged?

MAGHAZO
error herald.
he right hand of doom.

THE PRANK ADDICT
Remnant. Hospitalized. Faking amnesia.

RAYMOND & REGGIE
Bodyguards. Bruisers. Eyeballs.

SHEILA
Performer. Provocative. Parent.

ALBERT EISENHOWER

THE BONE COLLECTOR

SKYSCRAPER
Break muscle. Big.

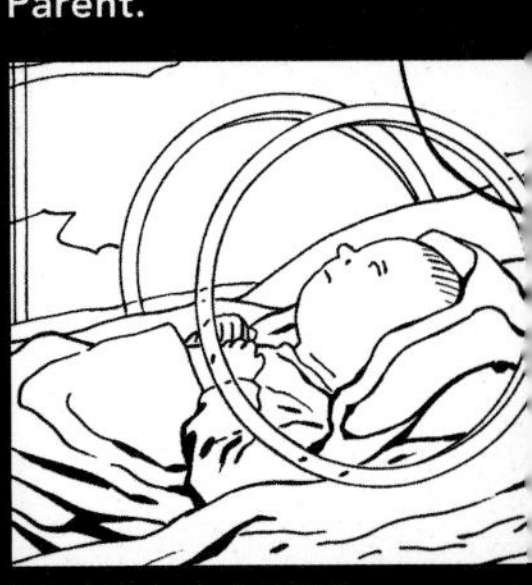

NEW BABY
Name unknown.

原作 JOE CASEY

漫画 PIOTR KOWALSKI

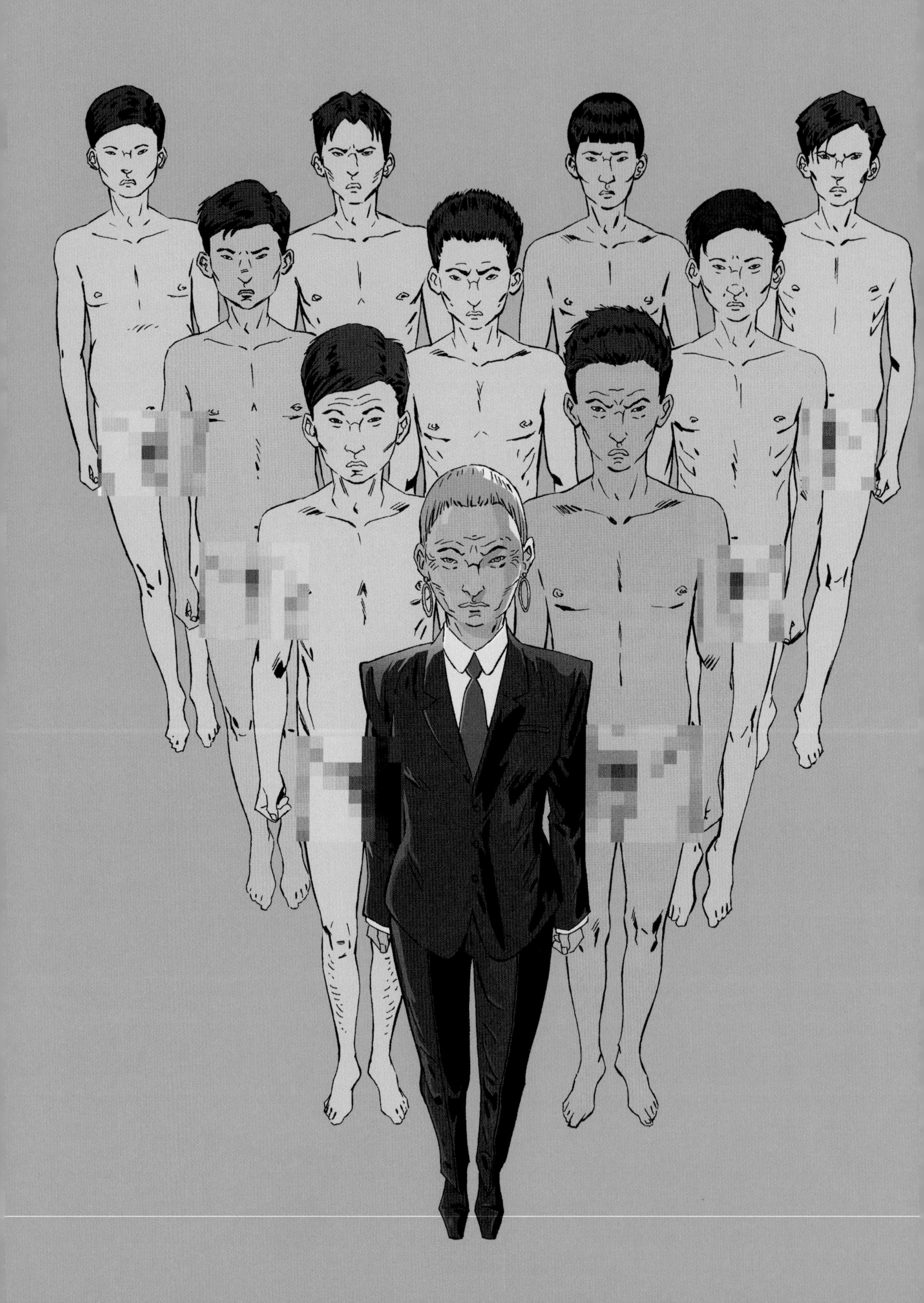

SEX™
風俗

CHAPTER TWENTY-SEVEN

REFLEXOLOGY

JOE CASEY WRITER · PIOTR KOWALSKI ARTIST · BRAD SIMPSON COLORIST · RUS WOOTON LETTERER · SONIA HARRIS GRAPHIC DESIGNER

E COOKE
MPANY:
WE'VE KNOWN EACH OTHER FOR LMOST TEN YEARS, RRY. I'VE WATCHED YOU GO FROM ASSISTANT TO EXECUTIVE IN RECORD TIME.
YOU'VE BECOME THE KIND OF CONFIDANT THAT I REALLY NEEDED HERE. WE BOTH KNOW I'M NOT A NATURAL AT THIS. I KNOW IT'S BEEN MORE THAN A LITTLE FRUSTRATING FOR YOU.
BUT THERE WAS A REASON FOR ALL OF IT. FOR A LONG TIME, THIS WHOLE THING WAS SIMPLY A MEANS TO AN END...
... I WAS DEALING WITH SOMETHING A LITTLE MORE INTENSE.
LITERALLY A DOUBLE-LIFE.
THE SATURN SENTINEL
THE NEWS OF THE CITY SINCE 1851
ARMORED SAINT FOILS DOWNTOWN JEWEL HEIST
EWELRY STORE
AS YOU CAN IMAGINE, IT TOOK A LOT OF FOCUS ON MY PART. BUT THERE WAS A GREATER GOOD...

SO... YEAH. THERE IT IS.
MAYBE THIS EXPLAINS A LOT FOR YOU... I DON'T KNOW. I DO KNOW IT'S A SECRET I HAD TO KEEP AT THE TIME.
BUT NOW... I FEEL LIKE IT'S SOMETHING YOU SHOULD KNOW ABOUT ME. ABOUT MY LIFE.
MAYBE MOVING FORWARD, WE CAN...
LARRY...?
WHAT'S... THE MATTER WITH YOU...?
MMFF

LOOK, I KNOW THIS IS DIFFICULT TO PROCESS --
BWAH--!
UH-HAHAHA--!

WHAT...
WHAT THE HELL ARE YOU LAUGHING ABOUT?!
OH... AAAHHH...
... HAHAHAHA...!
... S-SORRY...

IT'S JUST...
... HEH... AHEM
UMMM... I'VE ACTUALL KNOWN THIS FOR YEARS, SIMON.

I MEAN... I KNEW YOU WERE THE ARMORED SAINT. PRETTY MUCH RIGHT FROM THE BEGINNING.
IS THAT SO...?
AND YOU NEVER TOLD ME.

OH MY GOD... WOW...
AHHH... WELL, I KNEW IT WAS IMPORTANT TO YOU. OTHERWISE, YOU WOULD'VE TOLD ME SOONER, RIGHT...?
BUT, HONESTLY, IT WAS MORE THAN THAT.

IT WAS IMPORTANT TO THE CITY. TO THE PEOPLE OF THIS CITY.
AS WEIRD AS IT WAS, I WASN'T GOING TO MESS WITH IT. IT WASN'T MY PLACE TO MESS WITH IT.

SO ALL THIS TIME I WAS RUNNING AROUND, BENDING OVER BACKWARDS TO MAINTAIN THIS...
... "ALTERNATIVE LIFESTYLE"?
IS THAT THE PHRASE YOU'RE LOOKING FOR?

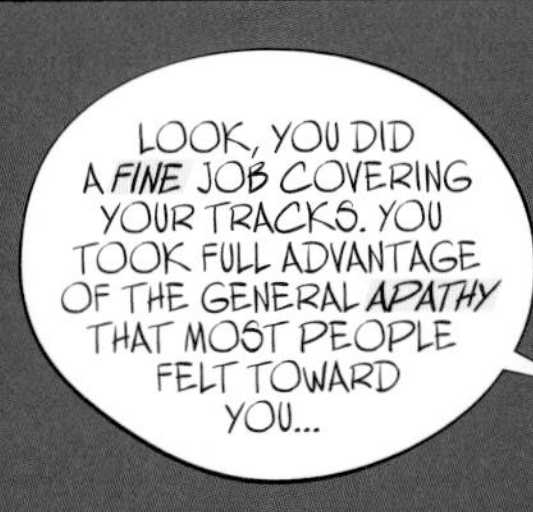

LOOK, YOU DID A *FINE* JOB COVERING YOUR TRACKS. YOU TOOK FULL ADVANTAGE OF THE GENERAL *APATHY* THAT MOST PEOPLE FELT TOWARD YOU...

... SOMETHING I'M SURE YOU *ENCOURAGED.*
BUT I WAS WATCHING A LITTLE *CLOSER...*

-- I KNOW THIS IS AN IMPORTANT VOTE, BUT I... HAVE A *LUNCH* THING I NEED TO GET TO...
IF YOU'LL *EXCUSE* ME...

WHAT HAPPENED TO YOUR *FACE,* MISTER COOKE...?
I... CUT MYSELF *SHAVING,* THAT'S ALL.

WHAT IS *THIS,* EXACTLY? FEELS *WARM...*
OH... SOMEONE FROM R&D LEFT THAT UP HERE.
THINK IT'S SOME SORT OF *CIGARETTE LIGHTER...*

... SO, *YEAH.* I FIGURED IT OUT.
IF I *HADN'T,* I WOULD HOPE YOU'D HAVE *FIRED* ME FOR BEING SO BLIND TO THE *OBVIOUS.*

WHEN YOU CAME *BACK,* I KNEW IT WAS OVER. YOU WERE DONE. SO WHY *PUSH* IT...?
THERE ARE STILL THINGS TO *DO.* AND YOU CAN DO THEM... RIGHT *HERE.*
YOU KNOW YOU CAN *TRUST* ME. SO LET'S JUST GET BACK TO *WORK,* OKAY...?

...
OKAY, THEN.

WASTE OF TIME...!

I DON'T THINK YOU'RE GETTING ME THERE, HONEY...
HEY, DREXLER --
MMMMMM...?
INSIDE SKIN
TERRITORY

-- SORRY TO INTERRUPT, BUT THIS IS IT. YOU NEED TO GET YOUR SHIT OVER TO THE CONCLAVE NOW.
THE BIG BULL'S READY FOR ANOTHER FACE-TO-FACE.

THINK HE'S FINALLY GONNA PULL THE TRIGGER ON THIS BITCH...?
CHRIST.
HE'D BETTER.

I KNOW YO
THINK YOU C
PLAY AT A
PRO LEVEL
DREX...

... BUT YOU ALSO KNOW THIS AIN'T NO GAME. YOU DON'T "PLAY" IT. YOU LIVE IT. THAT'S HOW YOU DOMINATE.
YOU'VE BEEN A FUCKING LOUDMOUTH LATELY. YOU THINK THE SKINS HAVE BEEN TOO CAUTIOUS AND YOU AIN'T BEEN SHY ABOUT SAYING IT.
I'M SICK OF IT. I WAS THINKING OF CUTTIN' YOU LOOSE...

... BUT INSTEAD, I'M GONNA GIVE YOU THE SHOT YOU BEEN MOANING ABOUT.
YOU WON'T REGRET THIS, BULLCHUCK.
THIS IS GONNA BE BIG.

DON'T WORRY ABOUT "BIG," ASSHOLE.
IF THIS THING DOESN'T GO OFF CLEAN...

... IT'S YOUR ASS.
KNOW WHAT I MEAN...?

FUCKIN' BULLCHUCK...
... ACTING LIKE HE'S DOING ME A FAVOR.
WHATEVER. WE'RE DOING THIS. AND IT'S GONNA BE GODDAMNED GLORIOUS.
HOW MANY SOLDIERS ARE WE GONNA NEED, DREX...?

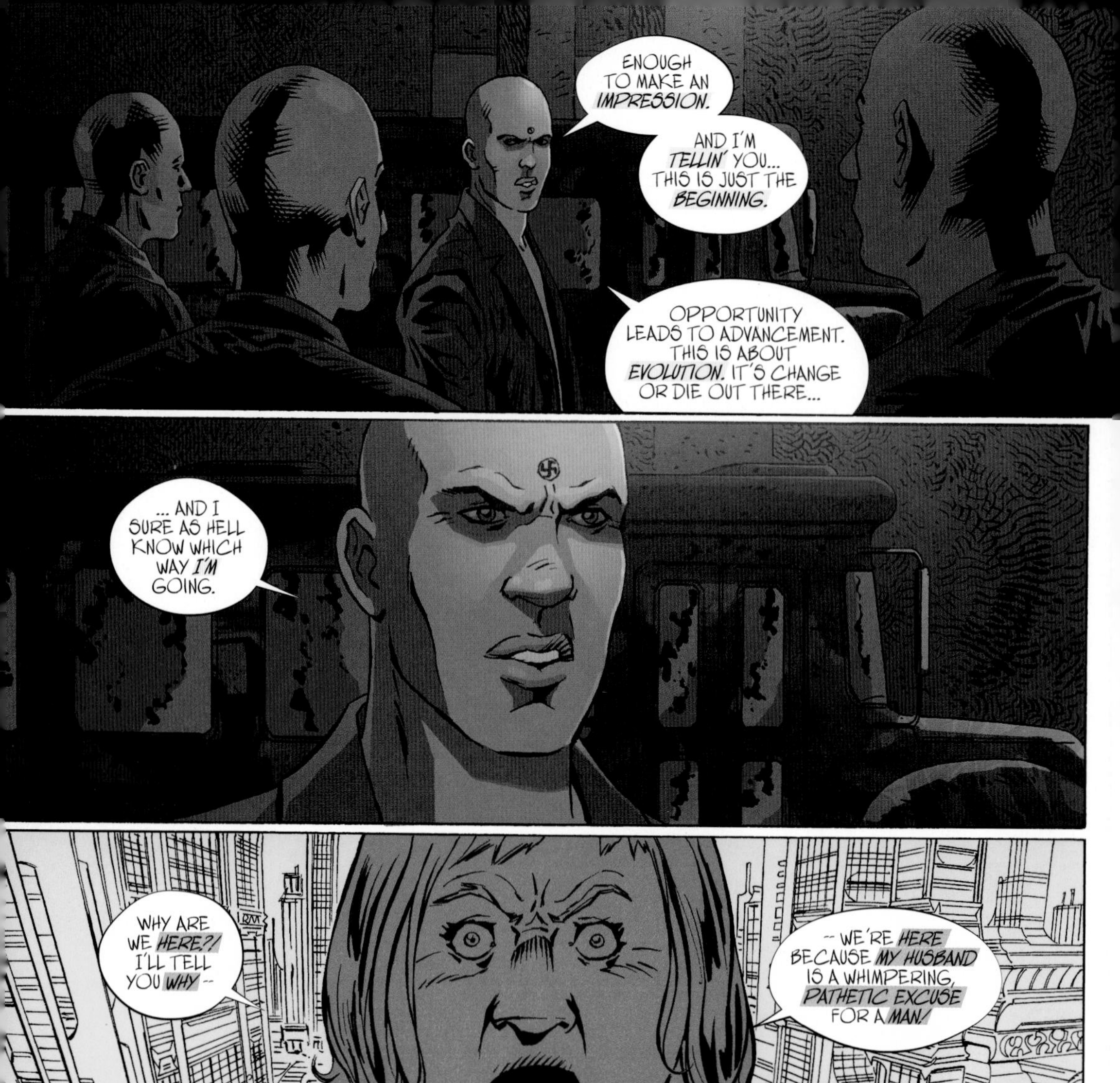
ENOUGH TO MAKE AN IMPRESSION.
AND I'M TELLIN' YOU... THIS IS JUST THE BEGINNING.
OPPORTUNITY LEADS TO ADVANCEMENT. THIS IS ABOUT EVOLUTION. IT'S CHANGE OR DIE OUT THERE...
... AND I SURE AS HELL KNOW WHICH WAY I'M GOING.

WHY ARE WE HERE?! I'LL TELL YOU WHY --
-- WE'RE HERE BECAUSE MY HUSBAND IS A WHIMPERING, PATHETIC EXCUSE FOR A MAN!

I MEAN, LOOK AT HIM! IT'S LIKE HE'S BARELY AWAKE!
HE HASN'T BEEN GOING TO WORK! HE'S GOT A PERVERTED MIND! I CAUGHT HIM ABUSING HIMSELF IN BED NEXT TO ME!
HE NEEDS TO GET HIS SHIT TOGETHER -- OR ELSE!
MARRIAGE COUNSELING:

HE HAS NO IDEA HOW LUCKY HE IS TO HAVE ME! HE SHOULD BE ON HIS KNEES WORSHIPPING THE GROUND I WALK ON!
I MEAN, WHAT WOULD YOU DO IF YOU HAD TO DEAL WITH SUCH A SAD WASTE OF SPACE DAY IN, DAY OUT...?!
WELL, BEVERLY, SINCE YOU ASKED...
... I THINK ELLIOT MAY BE DEALING WITH CIRCUMSTANCES QUITE NORMAL FOR MEN OF HIS AGE GROUP.
THE ROLE OF THE MALE PARTNER IN MODERN RELATIONSHIPS HAS BECOME MORE AND MORE CONFUSING... ESPECIALLY FOR THE MALE HIMSELF.
THERE IS THAT SENSE OF FEELING TRAPPED IN A ROLE HE IS ILL-EQUIPPED TO PLAY. AND SO THEY REACT IN VARIOUS WAYS.
WHAT DO YOU THINK, ELLIOT...?
ELLIOT...?

YOU'VE REACHED LORRAINE BAINES AT THE COOKE COMPANY --

-- PLEASE LEAVE A MESSAGE AT THE BEEP.
BEEP!
LARRY... I'M AT WORK, SO I CAN'T REALLY TALK. BUT I WANTED TO SEE IF WE COULD GET TOGETHER...
I-I KNOW THE LAST TIME WE SPOKE WAS AWKWARD AS HELL --
TUCKER --

-- YOU READY?
EVEN THOUGH IT'S STRICTLY ON THE DOWN LOW, SEDGWIC WANTS US IN HIS OFFIC WHILE HE GETS AN UPDATE FROM ONE OF HIS POLICE CONTACTS...

... THIS IS SOMETHING OCCURRING OUTSIDE OF THE CURRENT CONFLICTS PLAYING OUT BETWEEN THE VARIOUS, ACTIVE CRIMINAL ORGANIZATIONS.
AND AT A PRETTY STEADY CLIP FOR THE PAST FEW WEEKS.
THIS IS NOT THE NEWS I NEEDED TO HEAR, MCGREGOR...

... I'VE GOT ENOUGH PROBLEMS TRYING TO HOLD THIS CITY TOGETHER TO HAVE TO DEAL WITH THIS WILD CARD.
BEEN AWHILE SINCE THIS CASE WAS OPEN --

-- AND IT DOESN'T LOOK LIKE SHE'S LOST ANY OF HER MOJO, DOES IT?

SO, WHAT ARE THEY SAYING ABOUT IT IN THE DEPARTMENT...?
NOT MUCH AT THE MOMENT.
YOU KNOW HOW IT IS DOWN THERE... EVERYONE'S WAITING TO SUSS OUT WHO'S ON THE TAKE FROM WHOM. NO ONE KNOWS WHERE THIS FITS.
YOU'RE ONE OF THE FEW HONEST COPS LEFT, DETECTIVE. I KNOW IT'S A RISK FOR YOU TO EVEN BE HERE AND I APPRECIATE THAT.
GET ME MORE INTEL WHEN YOU CAN.
AND... COULD YOU CLOSE THE DOOR ON YOUR WAY OUT...?
YES, OF COURSE, SIR.
THAT WAS OMINOUS...
IF THE COMMISSIONER FINDS OUT THAT YOU'VE GOT FOLKS ON HIS PAYROLL SLIPPING YOU INFO...
THAT'S THE LEAST OF MY CONCERNS RIGHT NOW. BESIDES, THEY'RE ALL CIVIL SERVANTS, AREN'T THEY? JUST LIKE WE ARE.
TALK TO ME, TUCKER.
WELL, MISTER MAYOR...
... THIS MEETING YOU'RE COORDINATING BETWEEN MISTER WEBER AND SIMON COOKE IS DAMN NEAR CONFIRMED.
PERSONALLY, I'D RATHER DEAL WITH A CORRUPT POLICE PRECINCT THAN WHOEVER WEBER'S HOOKED UP WITH...
YOU HAVE NO IDEA.
LET'S JUST DO OUR PART... MAKE THIS LOVE CONNECTION... AND BE FUCKING DONE WITH IT.

It's weird how life goes on...
... and how much you can get away with.
ARE YOU SURE WE SHOULDN'T CALL THE POLICE...?
YOU WANNA RISK IT?! GO AHEAD...
It goes to show how the balance of power has shifted in this city. Masai's vision of respect is happening...
... even if it is hard-won.
HOW LONG DO YOU PEOPLE THINK YOU CAN POSSIBLY TAKE ADVANTAGE OF --
"YOU PEOPLE"?! DON'T EVEN THINK ABOUT IT, WHITE BOY...
... JUST KEEP A CLOSE EYE ON SHEILA AND THE KID AN' KEEP YO' MOUTH SHUT.
I'm here to make sure things don't get out of hand.

In the meantime, I'm using the opportunity to catch up on my reading...
It didn't take long at all for the truth to bear out. Even after just a few missions...

... Simon went along with it. But I should've known he wouldn't play well with others. Not in these games.
There was some success, no doubt about it. More boots on the ground -- especially when they're as capable as Keenan's -- was always going to be more effective.

on a personal level, the two of
simply didn't gel. And now, with
benefit of hindsight, I can see
.. at least from Simon's side.
He knew -- as I did -- that Keenan was simply better at this job than he was. His temperament was better suited for the lifestyle.
He was a natural.
So now I had another problem.
How long before this "partnership" completely imploded?

To his credit, Keenan never blinked. He knew there was important work to be done. He had his moments, no doubt about it. The Armored Saint's rogues gallery certainly weren't going to welcome him into the community without a requisite hazing period. But he hung in there.
And slowly but surely, I realized I might have a chance to set right this wayward ship... and do what I'd originally set out to do.
But I was running out of time --
SO THIS ISN'T TOO TERRIBLY CLICHED, IS IT...?
... NEW MOM BY DAY, ENTERTAINER BY NIGHT. AND HER LONG-SUFFERING EMPLOYER STOPPING BY TO CHECK UP ON HER...
Wait... I know that voice...
SINCE WHEN DID YOU SIGN UP THE BREAKS FOR ROUND-THE-CLOCK SECURITY...?
SHE'S SLEEPING, YO...
... BUT I'LL TELL HER YA' STOPPED BY.
YEAH, YOU DO THAT...
UHHH... HOLD ON...
Oh shit.
I knew when I got myself into this mess that I'd eventually have to deal with certain worlds colliding...
... I just never imagined which worlds.
KEENAN...?!

YOSHIKO-SAMA --

-- MAY I BE THE FIRST TO WELCOME YOU TO SATURN CITY?
I TRUST YOUR TRIP WAS WITHOUT INCIDENT. WE'VE BEEN LOOKING FORWARD TO YOUR VISIT.
I'M SIMON COOKE.

D I'M EALLY OPING YOUR GLISH S --
I KNOW WHO YOU ARE, MISTER COOKE. AND MY ENGLISH IS FINE.
I WOULD PREFER TO DISPENSE WITH THE PLEASANTRIES.
I WOULD LIKE TO GO IMMEDIATELY TO THE ROOM WHERE MY HUSBAND DIED.

UMMM... WITH ALL DUE RESPECT...

... WOULDN'T YOU BE MORE COMFORTABLE IN ONE OF THE OTHER SUITES YOU SECURED FOR THIS VISIT?
I MEAN, THIS IS --
THOSE ARE FOR MY STAFF, MISTER COOKE. SPEAKING OF WHICH...

... I WOULD LIKE TO BE ALONE WITH MISTER COOKE.
RIGHT NOW.
AHEM
I'M... SENSING SOME TENSION THERE --
THEY ARE SLOW TO ADJUST TO THE NEW PARADIGM.
THEY ARE STILL QUITE LOYAL TO MY LATE HUSBAND...
... AND HIS METHODS OF DOING BUSINESS.
BUT I AM NOT HERE TO SIMPLY DO BUSINESS.
I AM HERE TO SEE FOR MYSELF THE LEGACY OF SHAME...

... THE ASSAULT ON MY HONOR.
YOU KNEW WHAT OCCURRED HERE...
... DIDN'T YOU, MISTER COOKE...?
ONLY... AFTER THE FACT, I ASSURE YOU.

I SEE.
I HAVE ENDURED THIS CULTURE OF SILENCE FOR LONG ENOUGH...
... THE TIME HAS COME FOR ME TO ACT.

SINCE TAKING OVER MY HUSBAND'S COMPANY, I HAVE BEGUN TO FEEL MY POWER.
IT IS CONSIDERABLE. I HAVE COME INTO MY OWN.

AND NOW... I TAKE WHAT I WANT.
THE PLEASURES OF THE FLESH...

... NO LESS THAN ANY OF US DESERVE.
AHHHH, OKAY...
LISTEN...

I REALIZE MUST'VE PUT WITH A LOT. OUSLY, THIS 'T HIS FIRST OFFENSE.
BUT... I'M ST NOT SURE AT THIS IS THE HT CHOICE IF 'RE LOOKING FOR SOME SORT OF TISFACTION.
FOR ONE THING, I'M KIND OF... TAKEN...

I SEE.
SO YOU POSSESS A DEGREE OF HONOR.

BUT I NEED MINE RESTORED.
AND I NEED IT RIGHT HERE... RIGHT NOW...

WARREN!
CAN YOU POP IN HERE FOR A FEW MINUTES...?

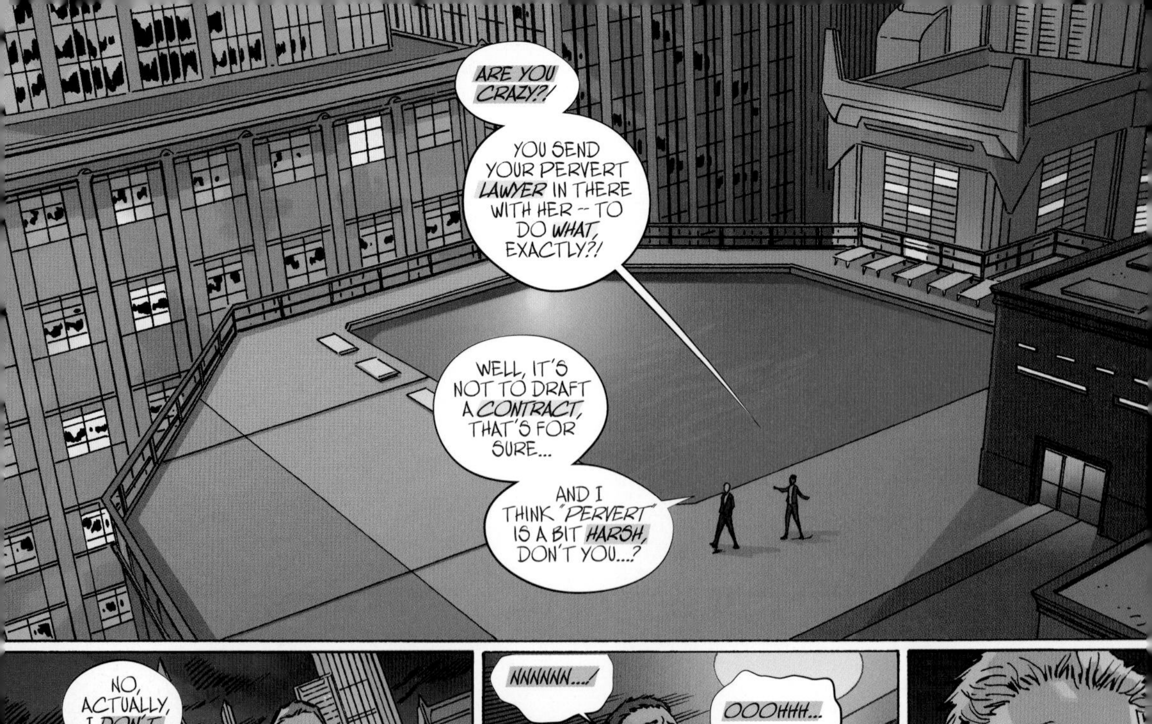
ARE YOU CRAZY?!
YOU SEND YOUR PERVERT LAWYER IN THERE WITH HER -- TO DO WHAT, EXACTLY?!
WELL, IT'S NOT TO DRAFT A CONTRACT, THAT'S FOR SURE...
AND I THINK "PERVERT" IS A BIT HARSH, DON'T YOU...?

NO, ACTUALLY, I DON'T.
I KNOW WHAT HE'S CAPABALE OF! AND HE'S ALONE IN THERE WITH THAT SAD, OLD WOMAN?! WHAT SHOULD I ASSUME IS HAPPENING--?!

NNNNNN...!
OOOHHH...
AAAAHHH--!

"SAD OLD WOMAN"? OH, I REALLY DON'T THINK SO, LARRY...
HONESTLY, I'D BE A LITT MORE WORR ABOUT WARR

< DO NOT... HOLD BACK... >
< STAKE YOUR CLAIM... DEEP WITHIN ME...! >
< DO IT, FAT ONE--! >*
* - TRANSLATED FROM JAPANESE
S-SORRY... I DON'T SPEAK JAPANESE...!

OMIGOD. THIS IS UNBELIEVABLE...!
I MEAN, IF THIS REALLY HOW YOU DO BUSINESS, THEN I'M NOT SURE I BELONG HERE ANYMORE...!

I THINK I LIKED IT BETTER BEFORE... WHEN YOU DIDN'T THINK THAT I...
HEY! WHAT'RE YOU LOOKING AT...?

I'M NOT SURE.
SOMETHING HAPPENING DOWN BEHIND THE HOTEL...

... I THINK SOMEONE MAY BE CRASHING THE PARTY.

WHAT DO YOU MEAN...?
SOMETHING ELSE I DIDN'T TELL YOU... WE DID A LITTLE DIGGING INTO WHAT REALLY HAPPENED WITH TANAKA AND HIS UNTIMELY PASSING.
THE... UMM... WOMEN THAT WERE HIRED -- AND KILLED -- WERE OWNED BY THE SKINS.

LOOKS LIKE THEY MIGHT'VE SHOWN UP TO SETTLE THE SCORE --
HEY! HOLD ON A MINUTE!
YOU'RE TALKING ABOUT THE STREET GANG, RIGHT?
OKAY, I DON'T KNOW IF THIS IS JUST OLD HABITS DYING HARD, BUT WHATEVER "ACTION" YOU'RE CONSIDERING... MAYBE DIAL IT BACK.
THIS ISN'T YOUR JOB ANYMORE. BESIDES...
... THERE'S GOT TO BE SOME OTHER WAY OUT OF THIS, RIGHT...?

< I WANT MY HONOR, BEAST-MAN! >
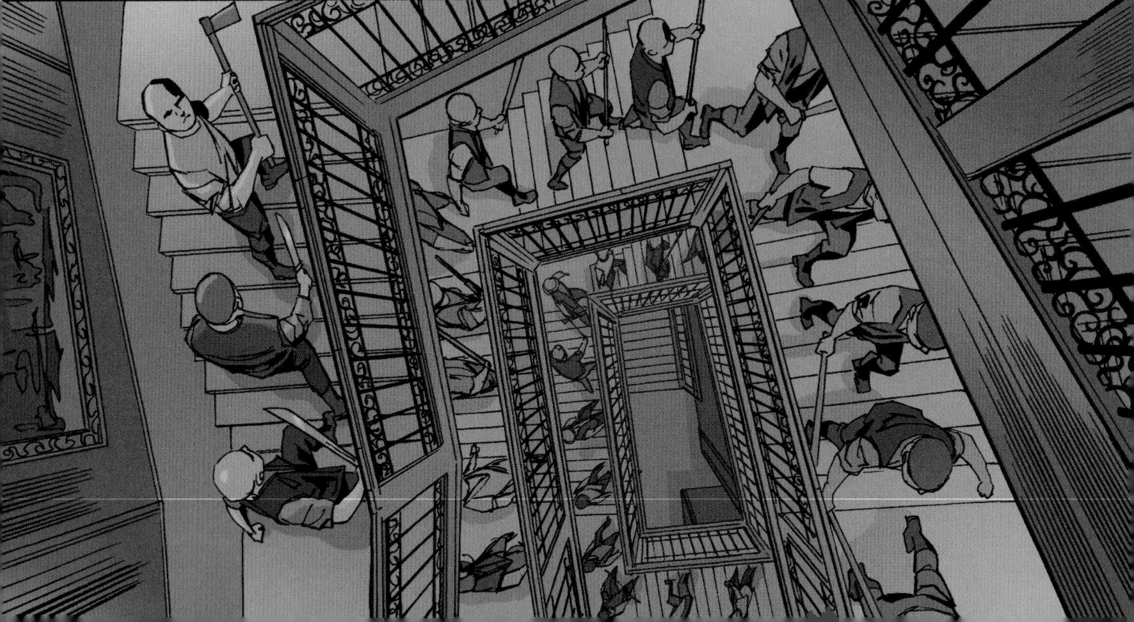

WITHIN THIS ISSUE:
A DARING ESCAPE
A HEROIC ACT
A DESPERATE GAMBIT
INFORMATION UNCOVERED
GOOGLING TRUTH
A SURPRISE CONFRONTATION

SEX™

CHAPTER TWENTY-EIGHT
PARTING THE RED SEA

JOE CASEY WRITER · PIOTR KOWALSK ARTIST · BRAD SIMPSON COLORIST · RUS WOOTON LETTERER · SONIA HARRIS GRAPHIC DESIGNER

QUITE A SCENE UP THERE, KEENAN.
PREEMIE BIRTH. SOME HEALTH COMPLICATIONS. GANG MEMBERS STANDING GUARD AT THE DOOR...
I'M JUST TRYING TO HELP. SHEILA IS SKYSCRAPER'S GIRL. AS FOR THE KID...
IMMATURE RESPIRATORY SYSTEM. PATENT DUCTUS ARTERIOSUS. RISK OF INTRAVENTRICULAR HEMORRHAGE.
SERIOUS SHIT. WE'RE IMBEDDED UNTIL THEY GIVE THEM BOTH THE ALL CLEAR.
RIGHT. WELL, THAT'S ADMIRABLE.
YOU KNOW, SHEILA WORKS FOR ME. SHE'S WAY DEEP IN THAT WORLD. SO GOD ONLY KNOWS WHO THE FATHER IS...
DOESN'T MATTER. KID'S HERE NOW. THAT'S HOW IT GOES.
NOW LET'S CUT THE SHIT, ANNABELLE. I MADE YOU THE MOMENT YOU WALKED INTO THE ROOM.
BROUGHT BACK A LOT OF MEMORIES...

... I HAVEN'T HEARD MUCH OUTTA YOU IN THE LAST YEAR OR SO.
DID YOU RETIRE, TOO?
AND NOW WHAT... YOU BRING ME OUT HERE FOR SOME SORT OF COSTUME CLASS REUNION?
LOOKS LIKE YOU'RE ALREADY WEARING A NEW COSTUME --
OKAY, WE'RE DONE HERE.
I'M DOING WHAT I'M SUPPOSED TO BE DOING. YOU DON'T HAVE A FUCKING CLUE ABOUT IT.
IF YOU'RE RUNNING WITH THE BREAKS NOW, I THINK I HAVE SOME CLUE ABOUT IT, KID.
WAS BEING A FAILED SIDEKICK SO TRAUMATIC THAT YOU HAD TO SWITCH SIDES...?
FUCK YOU. GO BACK TO THE FREIHEIT DISTRICT AND PEDDLE YOUR WARES THERE.
WHEN SHIT FINAL SHAKES O YOU'LL KNO EXACTLY W I'M UP TO
JUST MIND YOUR BUSINESS, "SHADOW LYNX".
XIT
SO... YOU GOT SOMETHING OR ARE WE SCREWED HERE?!
HOLD ON.
I'M STILL THINKING.

C'MON, SIMON... THE TOP FLOOR IS FILLED WITH ANSEI'S TOP BRASS --
-- NOT TO MENTION YOUR LAWYER'S SHTUPPING THE NEW CEO IN THE PENTHOUSE SUITE EVEN AS WE SPEAK!
OKAY...
... IT'LL TAKE AWHILE FOR THE SKINS TO GET UP HERE AND FIND WHAT THEY'RE LOOKING FOR.
CALL EDDIE WITH THE COMPANY COPTER. TELL HIM TO GET HIS ASS HERE ASAP.
I'LL BE RIGHT BACK.
AHEM
-- SORRY TO INTERRUPT YOU TWO.
BUT WE HAVE TO LEAVE.

SO, COME ON --
-- UP AN' AT 'EM.

QUICKLY, NOW... WE REALLY DON'T HAVE MUCH TIME HERE.
TRY AND KEEP IT ORDERLY...
SIMON! WHAT THE HELL IS GOING ON--?!

DON'T WORRY. WE'LL BE FINE.
AS YOU CAN SEE, I'VE GOT AIR TRANSPORT ARRIVING.

JUST GET READY TO MOVE.

YOU'RE SURE THIS IS THE WAY TO GO?!
IS EVERYONE GOING TO FIT IN HERE?!
ONLY ONE WAY TO FIND OUT...
KIDDING IT'LL BE TIGHT, BU IT SHOUL BE FINE...

ALRIGHT, YOU TWO... CLIMB IN --
IS THIS REALLY NECESSARY--?
TH-THIS IS... HIGHLY UNORTHODOX...!

YOSHIKO-SAMA. AS IF THIS EVENING WASN'T STRANGE ENOUGH...
BUT I IMPLORE YOU TO GET ON THIS HELICOPTER RIGHT NOW.
TRUST ME.

WATCH YOUR STEP.
IT'S CROWDED, I KNOW. JUST TRY TO MAKE ROOM...

... NO MATTER WHAT, Y'HEAR ME?
YES, SIR.

NG!
JEEZUS...!
SIMON! ARE YOU IN HERE?!

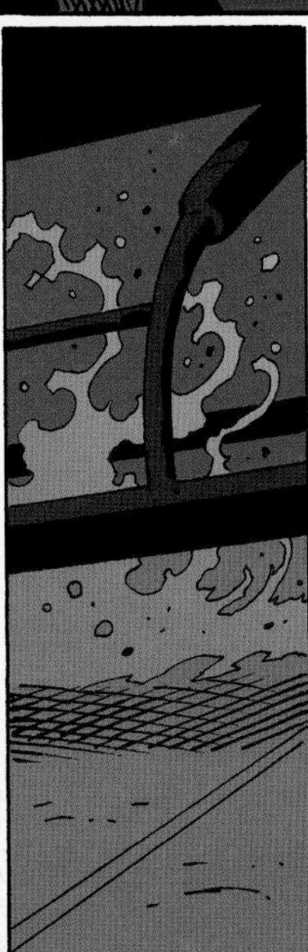

OH DAMN.
HATE TO BREAK IT TO YOU, LARRY...

... BUT IT LOOKS LIKE YOUR BOSS HAS GOT OTHER IDEAS.
OH MY GOD.
FOR CHRIST'S SAKE--!
EDDIE! WE NEED TO GO BACK! TURN THIS BIRD AROUND!
NO CAN DO, MISS BAINES. I'VE GOT STRICT ORDERS TO FLY US STRAIGHT BACK TO THE COOKE BUILDING...
... FROM MISTER COOKE HIMSELF.
WHAT'RE YOU DOING?
CALLING THE POLICE, THAT'S WHAT...

YOU READY TO FUCK SHIT UP?!
HELL, YES --

GODDAMMIT.
THOUGHT THIS PLACE WAS SUPPOSED T'BE FULL OF JAPS...!

DIDN'T DREXLER HAVE ROCK SOLID INTEL?!
DAMN STRAIGHT. UNLESS THIS IS SOME KIND OF --

-- AMBUSH...!
LET'S DANCE, ASSHOLES.

THE SATURN SENTINEL:
AHEM!
MISS JEMAS...?

CLAYTON.
TELL ME WE FINALLY HAVE A RESEARCH ASSISTANT THAT ACTUALLY DOES HIS JOB AROUND HERE...

WELL, I DUNNO... BUT I DID WHAT YOU ASKED AND LOOKED INTO THAT PHOTO YOU GAVE ME.
Y'KNOW, THE WOMAN WITH SIMON COOKE... OUTSIDE THE MANDALORIAN...
GREAT. HAVE A SEAT.

SO DID YOU FIND OUT WHO SHE IS? I MEAN, THAT'S THE WHOLE BALL GAME, CLAYTON...
W-WELL...

... IT CERTAINLY WASN'T EASY. A RANDOM PAPARAZZI PHOTO ISN'T A LOT TO GO ON. AND A PROFILE SHOT, EVEN...!
BUT I KNOW A GUY WHO KNOWS A GUY WHO'S INTO VIRTUAL FACIAL MAPPING AND RECOGNITION SOFTWARE. LIKE, CIA-LEVEL TECH...

... AND THAT WAS CROSS-REFERENCED WITH AN OLD PASSPORT PHOTO WE TURNED UP...
I LIKE WHERE THIS IS GOING.

S-SO... I THINK I HAVE A MATCH. BUT... I SHOULD WARN YOU --
OKAY, YOU'RE ACTING LIKE YOU'RE DEALING STATE SECRETS. OUT WITH IT.
IT'S JUST... I DUNNO... I'VE HEARD YOU DON'T LIKE IT WHEN THINGS GET...
I-I MEAN, THIS IS SOME REAL TABLOID FODDER --
CLAYTON... CLAYTON... GET A GRIP, KID...
... BELIEVE ME, I'M WELL AWARE THAT THIS PARTICULAR STORY HAS TAKEN ME PLACES I DID NOT WANT TO GO.
BUT I'M IN TOO DEEP NOW. AND THERE IS DEFINITELY SOMETHING WEIRD GOING ON WITH THE VENERABLE MISTER COOKE.
SO... WHO THE HELL IS SHE?
ALRIGHT, WELL... I'M PRETTY SURE SHE'S A NIGHTCLUB OWNER... IN THE, UMMM, FREIHEIT DISTRICT...
... BUT A... SPECIFIC TYPE OF NIGHTCLUB. ONE THAT SPECIALIZES IN... WELL...
... ADULT ENTERTAINMENT.
...
FUCK ME.

POLICE
...UUHHHHNN...
... WHAT... TOOK YOU SO LONG...?
... I THINK... I'M HURT...

I SEE YOUR SHOULDERS SLUMPING, ALBERT...
... DOES THAT MEAN YOU'VE GIVEN UP? YOU PULL UP A NAME LIKE "VIZ IBN ZIYAD" WITH NO FURTHER FOLLOW-UP AND EXPECT US TO ACCEPT THAT?
I DON'T THINK SO.
WE WANT TO KNOW WHO THIS MYSTERIOUS FUCKER IS... AND YOU'RE GONNA FIND OUT FOR US.
THAT'S WHAT YOU DO.
WUP -- HOLD THAT THOUGHT. THAT'S ME RINGING.
MY THINKS-HE'S-THE-BETTER-HALF CALLING IN FROM THE FIELD...
DOLPH.
WHAT A COINCIDENCE. I'M SITTING HERE WITH THE ONE AND ONLY OPERATOR AS HE CONTINUES HIS QUEST TO --
ENOUGH WITH THE SWEET TALK --

-- SHIT'S GETTING DRAMATIC OUT HERE.
THE WEST END WAREHOUSE GOT HIT HARD. WHOEVER THEY WERE... THEY AMBUSHED AN INCOMING SHIPMENT AS IT ROLLED INTO THE LOADING DOCK HERE...

SON OF A BITCH!
IT'S THE OLD MAN, ISN'T IT?! ALL OUR INTEL HAD HIM DOWN LIKE A BEATEN DOG --

-- BUT IT'S LIKE HE'S SUDDENLY STARTED TO FIGHT BACK!
THAT'S PUTTING IT MILDLY, CHA-CHA. THEY ALSO FIREBOMBED STOREFRONTS NEAR THE APPICE ON-RAMPS THAT WE WERE PROTECTING...!
CLEARLY, THE OLD MAN'S FINALLY READY TO GO TO WAR...

IT ALL FEELS SO GODDAMN DIFFERENT, RAY...

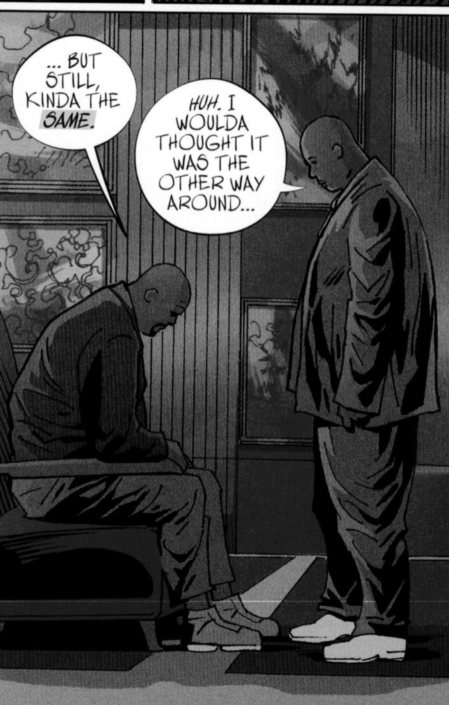
... BUT STILL, KINDA THE SAME.
HUH. I WOULDA THOUGHT IT WAS THE OTHER WAY AROUND...

LUCKILY, WE KNEW THE OLD MAN AS WELL AS ANYBODY.

... HE'D PUSH BACK.
LIKE A MOTHERFUCKER.
SHO' NUFF. MEANWHILE, I KNOW GABE'S STILL OUT THERE SWINGIN' HIS DICK AROUND.
YOU READY...?
LET'S DO IT.

... SO I STOOD UP... STARED HIM RIGHT IN HIS FUCKIN' EYES...
... TOLD HIM TO STEP THE FUCK OFF --
YOU A REAL BAD ASS, GABE...

... WHY DON'T YOU TELL MY BIG BLACK ASS TO STEP THE FUCK OFF?
H-HEY--!

WHU... WHAT'S THIS ALL ABOUT, FELLAS...?!
YOU'LL FIND OUT.
WE'RE GONNA NEE TO STEP INTO OUR OFFICE...

UGH--!

W-WAIT... DON'T --
LET'S TALK ABOUT THE STATE OF THE UNION.
SOMEONE'S TRYIN' TO BUTT IN ON THE BIG DANCE. LOTTA' NOISE HAPPENIN'. BUT HERE'S THE THING...
... THE OLD MAN WANTS TO KNOW WHO HE'S FIGHTIN', Y'DIG...?

FIGURE YOU'RE THE KINDA GUTTER RAT THAT CAN SNIFF THAT OUT FOR US, RIGHT, GABE...?
I-I DON'T KNOW NOTHIN' RAY... I JUST, Y'KNOW, HANG OUT ON THE PERIPHERY OF SHIT...

FUCK THAT. YOU GOT YER EAR TO THE GROUND. SO YOU JUST PUT THE WORD OUT...
... THE OLD MAN IS PISSED. AND WHEN HE GETS PISSED, SHIT GOES DOWN, Y'DIG?
NOW GET YER SKINN ASS OUTT HERE.

PANT!
PANT!
PANT!
I DON'T KNOW HOW LONG WE CAN KEEP THIS UP, RAY...

... I MEAN, HOW LONG BEFORE IT GETS OUT THE OLD MAN'S REALLY CROAKED...?
I DUNNO. BUT I BEEN THINKING...

... WE GOT US AN OPPORTUNITY HERE. WE MOVE QUICK ENOUGH, WE CAN FIND OUT WHO'S FUCKIN' WITH US AND SHUT 'EM DOWN BEFORE ANYONE KNOWS SHIT.
REMEMBER WHAT MOLINA SHOWED US? THE HORROR SHOW AT THE INDRA?

WHATCHA GOT THERE...?
JUST SOMETHING WE NEED TO GET OUR HANDS ON. AFTER ALL, IF THIS IS WAR...

... WE NEED OURSELVES A HELLUVA WEAPON, RIGHT?

THE AUSTRIAN ALPS:
THIS IS WEBER REPORTING IN.
I'M IN TELFS-BUCHEN RIGHT NOW.
SPECTACULAR VIEW, BY THE WAY.
SO DO YOU FEEL SECURITY WON'T BE AN ISSUE...?
NOT AT ALL. WE'VE DONE A COMPLETE SWEEP OF THE HOTEL AND EVERYTHING SEEMS CLEAN.
I'M CONFIDENT IN SAYING THAT THIS LOCATION WILL SERVE OUR NEEDS PERFECTLY...

... NOW, IF YOU DON'T MIND, I'D LIKE TO RETURN TO THE SIMON COOKE DISCUSSION.
I'M FLYING BACK TO SATURN CITY TOMORROW. A PERSONAL MEETING HAS FINALLY BEEN BROKERED FOR NEXT WEEK.
BE CAREFUL, MISTER WEBER...

... AS WE'VE TOLD YOU SEVERAL TIMES ALREADY, WE'RE ONLY MARGINALLY CONVINCED THAT COOKE IS EVEN WORTH TALKING TO.
THAT KANSEI MERGER SEEMS IMMINENT. OUR INTEL HAS HIM MEETING WITH THE LATE CEO'S WIFE EVEN AS WE SPEAK.

WELL, WE ALL KNOW WHAT A CATASTROPHE THAT MERGER WOULD BE. I'M CERTAIN THAT COOKE KNOWS IT, TOO.
BUT I'LL MAKE CERTAIN HE DOESN MAKE SUCH A RAS MOVE. AFTER ALL THERE ARE MUCH LARGER ISSUES AT STAKE HERE...

... THE FUTURE OF THE *HUMAN RACE,* FOR STARTERS.

I DON'T KNOW. SHE'S PRETTY *OUT* OF IT...

... AND THE *BABY'S* NOT OUT OF THE WOODS YET, EITHER. IT'S GRIM, REAL LIFE STUFF.
HAS ANYONE IN THE OFFICE LOOKED INTO SHEILA'S EMPLOYEE *HEALTH COVERAGE...?*
LEVEL 16 -D

NOT YET. HONESTLY, IT'S NOT EXACTLY STANDARD PROTOCOL TO *OFFER* A HEALTH PLAN AT A JOB LIKE THIS, MA'AM...
YOU CAN NOMINATE ME FOR SAINTHOOD *LATER,* RACHEL...

... FOR *NOW,* LET'S JUST MAKE SURE WE KNOW HOW SOMETHING THIS *DRASTIC* AFFECTS OUR OVERALL POLICY.
THIS IS ALL-NEW TERRITORY. WE'VE CERTAINLY NEVER HAD TO PAY FOR *MATERNITY LEAVE* BEFORE...!

YOU'RE A PIONEER, MISS LAGRAVENESE.
WHATEVER. FEELS MORE LIKE I'M JUST A --
OUTTA THE WAY --
-- COMING THROUGH, PEOPLE!
OKAY, WE GOT MULTIPLE FRACTURES... GSW'S... CONCUSSION... POSSIBLE BRAIN CONTUSIONS... PROBABLY SOME INTERNAL BLEEDING...
MOVE IT! THIS GUY GOT THE SHIT KICKED OUTTA HIM!
KEEP HIS C-SPINE STEADY! TELL 'EM TO PREP AN O.R. FOR IMMEDIATE SURGERY --
-- OTHERWISE WE MAY LOSE HIM!
OH DAMN...!

SEX

CHAPTER TWENTY-NINE
WHERE EAGLES DARE

JOE CASEY WRITER · PIOTR KOWALSKI ARTIST · BRAD SIMPSON COLORIST · RUS WOOTON LETTERER · SONIA HARRIS GRAPHIC DESIGNER

... NEVER LET 'EM SEE YOU SWEAT... NEVER LET 'EM SEE YOU SWEAT...
... EVERY MAJOR PROJECT GOES INTO OVERAGES... THAT'S HOW BUSINESS WORKS...
DREXLER.
HE'S READY FOR YOU.
HOPE YOU'RE WEARIN' A CUP, M'MAN...

SO, I GAVE YOU A SHOT, SLICK... A BIG FUCKIN' SHOT...
... A MAJOR OPERATION OUT IN THE OPEN. YOU WANTED IT OLD SCHOOL AND YOU GOT IT --

-- SO WHAT THE FUCK HAPPENED?!
I TOLD YOU I WANTED THIS CLEAN! BUT YOU COME BACK WITH SOLDIERS BEAT TO SHIT BY WHO KNOWS WHAT--!
AND THE ONES THAT DIDN'T COME BACK -- SOME OF 'EM PROBABLY IN CUSTODY! SOME OF 'EM PROBABLY DEAD!

IS THAT WHAT YOU SET OUT TO PROVE T'ME?! THAT YOU'RE A WORLD CLASS FUCK UP?!
UHHH... OF COURSE NOT, BOSS.
I-I'D JUST LIKE TO POINT OUT... IN BUSINESS, EVERY MAJOR PROJECT... GOES INTO OVERAGES --
WHOA! THIS AIN'T BUSINESS, DREXLER --

-- THIS IS PERSONAL!

YOU BEGGED ME FOR THIS!
NOW I GOTTA STEP UP AND FIGURE OUT WHAT'S NEXT, DON'T I...?
AHHHH...
... SHIT.

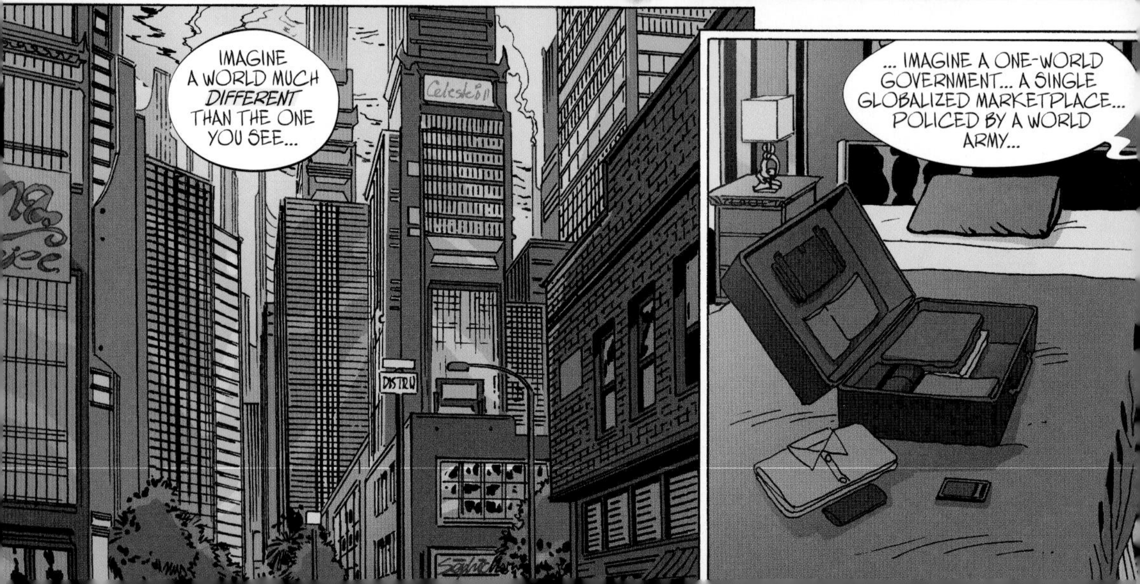

IMAGINE A WORLD MUCH DIFFERENT THAN THE ONE YOU SEE...
... IMAGINE A ONE-WORLD GOVERNMENT... A SINGLE GLOBALIZED MARKETPLACE... POLICED BY A WORLD ARMY...

... IMAGINE A SINGLE GLOBAL CURRENCY FINANCIALLY REGULATED BY A WORLD BANK...
... WE'VE BEEN BUILDING TO THIS POINT FOR MORE THAN SEVENTY YEARS...
THINK ABOUT IT, MISTER COOKE... WHO COULD'VE GOTTEN TO CHINA BEFORE NIXON DID...?
WHO CONTROLS OIL PRICES? WHO INFLUENCES WORLD LEADERS? WHO GETS THEM IN AND OUT OF OFFICE...?
WE'RE GOING TO UNITE THE PLANET. AND WE WANT YOU TO BE A PART OF IT.
SO YOU HAVE A CHOICE TO MAKE --
ZZZZZT
ZZZZZT
THIS IS WEBER.
OF COURSE I'M IN SATURN CITY. THE MEETING WITH COOKE IS BEING ARRANGED THROUGH --
SORRY...
... HE'S WHERE...?!

YOU CAN'T POSSIBLY BE COMFORTABLE...
... THE NURSES TELL ME YOU'RE REFUSING YOUR PAIN MEDS. IS THAT WISE...?
NOT TO MENTION... WHAT THE HELL WERE YOU THINKING?!
I'M PRETTY SURE I'VE SQUARED THINGS WITH THE POLICE, SIMON. BUT THIS ISN'T LIKE THE OLD DAYS...
BELIEVE ME... I'M WELL AWARE...
IT WAS... DEFINITELY AN EYE-OPENER... SO TO SPEAK...
... BUT... WE LIVE AND LEARN, DON'T WE...?
JEEZUS, LET'S HOPE SO.
IF YOU FEEL YOU'RE LUCID ENOUGH TO HAVE THIS DISCUSSION, LET'S TALK ABOUT KANSEI...

.. NEEDLESS SAY, YOU NEVER OT AROUND TO KING BUSINESS 'H THE WIDOW TANAKA.
I MEAN... THAT WAS THE WHOLE PURPOSE OF HER VISIT, WASN'T IT...?
YOU'D... BE SURPRISED...
... AND STOP SULKING BACK THERE, WARREN...
L-LOOK... I'M JUST NOT SURE HOW TO... I DUNNO...
... I MIGHT'VE GOTTEN A LITTLE CARRIED AWAY...
HEY, I ASKED YOU... REMEMBER...? YOU DID EXACTLY WHAT THE SITUATION CALLED FOR...
I... SHOULD'VE KNOWN THE SKINS WOULD CRAWL OUT OF THEIR HOLE AND... WELL, ANYWAY...
... LET'S TALK ABOUT BUSINESS, THEN.

THERE WAS REASON I WANTED TO TALK TO ANAKA'S WIDOW FACE-TO-FACE...
... AND I STILL NEED TO RIP THAT BAND-AID OFF, DON'T I...?
AN UNPOPULAR OPINION IN YOUR OWN COMPANY, I MIGHT ADD. BUT IF YOU'RE DEAD SET AGAINST THE MERGER...
... THEN, YES, THAT CONVERSATION NEEDS TO HAPPEN. GIVEN THE CIRCUMSTANCES, YOU MIGHT WANT TO CONSIDER A PROXY TO --
NO... I CAN DO THIS...
... JUST GET HER UP HERE.

ALRIGHT, SETTLE DOWN...
SATURN CITY POLICE DEPARTMENT; 20th PRECINCT:
... MAYOR SEDGWICK'S HERE, SO LET'S GET THIS MEETING STARTED.
NOW WE AL KNOW THING HAVE BEEN A LIT FUCKED UP T PAST YEAR OR PARDON MY FRENCH...
... WE'RE TRYING TO QUELL A FULL-BLOWN TURF WAR AND WE DON'T EVEN KNOW THE SIDES THAT'RE FIGHTING IT.
ON TOP OF THAT, WE'VE GOT GANG VIOLENCE SPREADING LIKE WILDFIRE BEYOND ANYTHING WE'VE SEEN BEFORE... BUT WE'RE NOT HERE TO TALK ABOUT THOSE CHESTNUTS.
WE'VE GOT OURSELVES AN OLD SPARRING PARTNER BACK IN TOWN. SHE LIKES TO KILL AND SHE IS ON A ROLL...

HI.
I SAW YOU SITTING HERE ALL ALONE...
... LOOKING AT ME.

FIRST OF ALL, LET ME SAY THAT I APPRECIATE COMMISSIONER BERGER'S INVITE TO COME DOWN AND SPEAK TO YOU ALL PERSONALLY.
OBVIOUSLY, NONE OF US KNOW WHY SHE'S BACK... BUT SHE HASN'T BEEN SHY WHEN IT COMES TO DOING WHAT SHE DOES BEST...
YOU... UHHH... SURE WE SHOULD...
... I MEAN, OUT HERE...?
WELL, WHY NOT. ALTHOUG TO TELL YOU THE TRUTH...
... I DON'T USUALLY DO THIS.

WE'RE LOOKING AT FATALITIES IN THE DOUBLE-DIGITS NOW. SO WE NEED TO PUT THE HAMMER DOWN.
WE KNOW HER M.O. WE KNOW HOW SHE OPERATES. SEEMS SIMPLE TO ME...
WE'VE GOT UNDERCOVER OFFICERS ALREADY TROLLING THE BARS DOWNTOWN...
WHU...?
WHAT IS THAT...?!
HOPEFULLY, WE'LL GET LUCKY AND SHE'LL TARGET AT LEAST ONE OF THEM.
I'M SURE YOU FELLAS WILL BE RIGHT THERE TO MAKE YOUR MOVE IF SHE DOES...

I THINK WE ALL KNOW THIS IS A CHANCE TO PROVE THAT SATURN'S IN GOOD HANDS... EVEN WITHOUT ITS GUARDIAN ANGEL.
SO DON'T FUCK THIS UP.

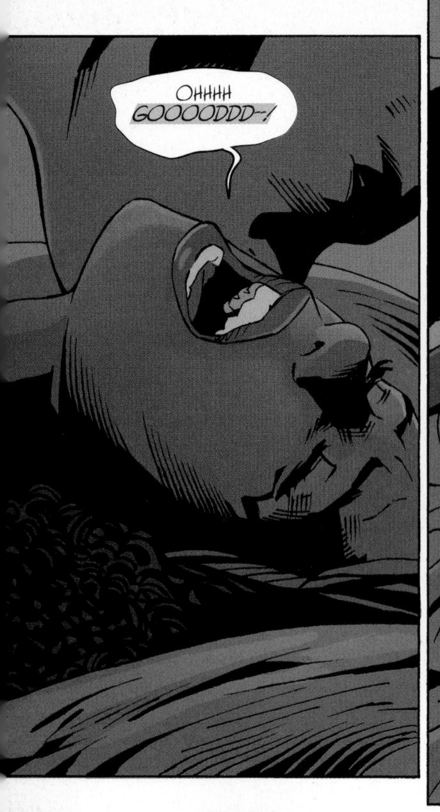
OHHHH GOOOODDD--!

KEENAN... KEENAN... KEENAN...
RIGHT THERE... RIGHT THERE...
OOOHHHH --
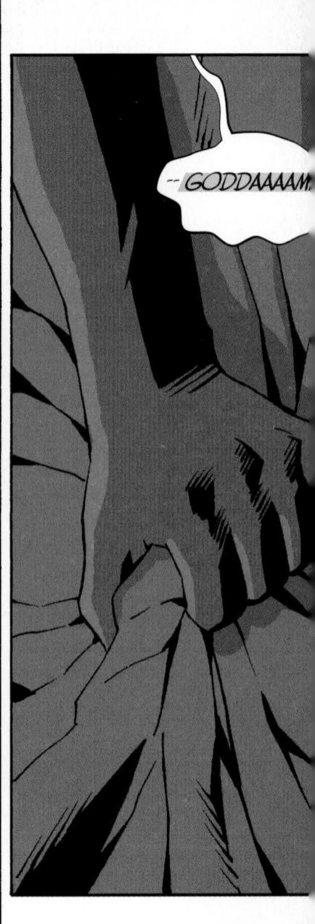
--GODDAAAAM

WHEW...!
YOU ARE IN RARE FORM, Y'KNOW THAT?
SO... DOES LIVIN' ON THE EDGE MAKE YOU MORE SEXUALLY POTENT OR WHAT...?

I WOULDN'T KNOW, BABY... THIS AIN'T EXACTLY THE EDGE.
MAYBE I'M JUST A LITTLE MORE SELF-ACTUALIZED LATELY...

...AND I'M LEARNING NEW THINGS EVERY DAY.

WHAT'S THAT...?!
REMEMBER THE BUS LOCKER KEY? THIS IS WHAT WAS IN THE LOCKER...
... I GUESS IT'S KIND OF A MEMOIR. BUT, I DUNNO, IT'S MORE THAN THAT, TOO.
HMMM... ARE YOU IN IT?
YOU COULD SAY THAT, YEAH.
TURNS OUT... EVEN OLD FRIENDS LONG GONE CAN STILL SURPRISE YOU.

Y, I'M JUST YOUR LFRIEND, RIGHT? WHY NOT BE CRYPTIC AS FUCK...
... C'MON NOW. I DON'T WANNA PLAY THESE GAMES ANYMORE. I THOUGHT WE WERE IN THIS TOGETHER.
THAT'S WHAT I WANT, ANYWAY. BUT IF YOU CAN'T BE STRAIGHT WITH ME --
IT'S NOT LIKE THAT, VERNITA...
... THIS KINDA SHIT IS BIGGER THAN BOTH OF US. BUT YOU'RE RIGHT.
IT'S PAST TIME YOU KNEW THE WHOLE STORY.
ESPECIALLY NOW THAT I FINALLY DO.

LICE

LET'S G
GIRLFRIEN

... YOU DON'T WANNA BE HANGIN' AROUND HERE ANY LONGER THAN YOU HAVE TO. BESIDES, SOMEONE WANTS TO TALK T'YOU...
UNLESS, Y'KNOW, YOU WANNA GET PINCHED...

COME RE YOU... S YOU UESTED, STER OKE...
... NORMALLY, I WOULD NOT GRANT SUCH REQUESTS.
I'M SURE YOU WOULDN'T.
BUT... I AM ASHAMED. I CAME HERE TO REGAIN MY HONOR.
I FEEL I HAVE DONE EXACTLY THE OPPOSITE.
YOUR COUNTRY... YOUR CULTURE... IS A CURIOUS ONE. WHAT IT CANNOT EASILY CO-OPT... IT CORRUPTS. MY HONORABLE HUSBAND...
... IN HIS DEEPEST HEART, HE WANTED SO MUCH TO BE A PART OF THAT CULTURE. I WONDER WHETHER HE WAS INDEED CO-OPTED... OR WILLINGLY CORRUPTED.
SO I ASK MYSELF, NOW THAT I WALK IN HIS SHOES...
... WHAT SHALL BE MY FATE...?
IF IT HELPS... MY ATTORNEY HAD NOTHING BUT GOOD THINGS TO SAY ABOUT YOU.
IF HELPS NOT AT ALL.
BESIDES, I REALIZE NOW THAT MY HUSBAND'S ACTIONS WERE BEYOND THE PARAMETERS -- AND THE MORALITY -- OF OUR UNION, SUCH AS IT WAS.

I FEEL... MUCH CLOSER TO HIM IN DEATH THAN I EVER DID IN LIFE.
BUT THE COST OF SUCH SELF-KNOWLEDGE IS A HEAVY PRICE TO PAY, DON'T YOU THINK...?
I AM LEFT WITH THE... UNCERTAINTY ABOUT THE RELATIONSHIP BETWEEN BUSINESS AND HONOR.
MY HUSBAND HAD A VISION THAT YOU AND HE --
YOSHIKO-SAMA...
... LET'S NOT PRETEND... THAT YOU OWE HIM ANYTHING.
INSTEAD... HOW ABOUT WE DEAL WITH THE HERE AND NOW...
... I DON'T THINK EITHER ONE OF US WANTS TO CONTINUE ON THIS PATH, DO WE...?
ARE YOU SAYING... THE MERGER IS NO LONGER OF INTEREST...?
AT FIRST... I THOUGHT IT MIGHT BE AN EASY WAY OUT...
... BUT THERE ARE THINGS ABOUT MY COMPANY... THAT ARE ALMOST TOO COMPLEX... FOR ANYONE TO COPE WITH...
... AND LATELY I'VE REALIZED... NO ONE ELSE CAN...
... BESIDES, IT'S NOT EXACTLY MY COMPANY TO MERGE... NOT REALLY...

'M NOT
RE I FULLY
ERSTAND...
THAT'S OKAY. YOU DON'T HAVE TO...
...THAT PART'S ALL ON ME.
BY THE WAY... DID I TELL YOU HOW MUCH BETTER YOUR ENGLISH IS THAN MY JAPANESE...?
E FREIHEIT DISTRICT:

... YOU CAN CALL ME ANY NAME YOU WANT...
OKAY, THEN. MONEY WELL SPENT...

MISS JEMAS --

-- SORRY TO MAKE YOU WAIT.
SHE'LL SEE YOU NOW. IF YOU'D FOLLOW ME...
SURE.
YOU ARE TAKING ME TO HER OFFICE, RIGHT...?

I'VE READ YOUR WORK IN THE SENTINEL. YOU'RE THE REAL THING.
DON'T TELL ME YOU'VE STOOPED TO WRITING EXPOSES ON WHAT CONSENTING ADULTS DO TO GET THEIR ROCKS OFF...

... THIS IS A LEGITIMATE BUSINESS ENTERPRISE. SO IF YOU'RE LOOKING TO SOMEHOW DRAG MY NAME THROUGH THE MUD --
ACTUALLY, MISS LAGRAVENESE...

... YOU ONLY CONCERN ME INSOFAR AS I'M INTERESTED IN THE COMPANY YOU KEEP.
YOU PERSONALLY AREN'T EXACTLY HIGH PROFILE, BUT YOUR SOCIAL LIFE --
I SEE...

... AGAIN, NOT WHAT I EXPECTED BASED WHAT I'VE READ FROM YOU.
LET'S TAKE A LITTLE WALK, SHALL WE...?

AS YOU CAN SEE, WHAT WE PROVIDE HERE IS MERELY A FORM OF ENTERTAINMENT, MAINLY FOR UPSCALE PROFESSIONALS SEEKING REFUGE FROM THE MYRIAD STRESSES OF THE CITY.
RIGHT...
MY EMPLOYEES ARE PROTECTED. THEY'RE RESPECTED. IN RETURN, THEY'RE EXPECTED TO CONDUCT THEMSELVES AS COMPLETE PROFESSIONALS.
THIS IS ALL VERY INTERESTING, BUT I REALLY --
SO... A PHOTO OF ME STANDING OUTSIDE THE MANDALORIAN SENT YOU RACING DOWN HERE. VERY STRANGE.

CONSIDERING I DON'T GET OUT THAT MUCH --
AS I SAID, I'M MORE INTRIGUED BY WHO YOU WERE WITH.

YES, I GATHERED THAT.
BUT IT'S NOT EXACTLY NEWS, IS IT?

WELL, THAT DEPENDS, DOESN'T IT? I'M NOT GOING TO SPECULATE ON THE RELATIONSHIP BETWEEN YOU AND YOUR DINNER DATE.
BUT HE DOES HAVE A PECULIAR HISTORY WHEN IT COMES TO WOMEN...
OH, YOU HAVE NO IDEA...!

THAT'S WHY I'M HERE. YOU MIGHT BE THE ONLY ONE I'VE SPOKEN TO THAT CAN GIVE ME SOME ACTUAL INSIGHT INTO --
LET ME STOP YOU RIGHT THERE...

... I CAN APPRECIATE YOUR TENACITY. BUT YOU HAVEN'T "SPOKEN" TO ME. LET'S BE CLEAR ABOUT THAT.

OFF THE RECORD... YOU'RE POKING A BEAR THAT YOU DON'T WANT TO WAKE UP.

THIS CITY CONTAINS ITS SHARE OF SHADOWS. THE FOLKS WHO LIVE IN THEM... THEY DON'T WANT YOUR KIND OF LIGHT.
LOOK AROUND. MAYBE YOU'LL UNDERSTAND WHAT I'M TALKING ABOUT.
YOU CAN SEE YOURSELF OUT, I'M SURE...

OH, COME ON...!

ARE YOU... COMFORTABLE...?
LISTEN, I CAN... TALK TO THE DOCTORS. FIND OUT EXACTLY WHAT OUR OPTIONS ARE --
OH STOP IT...
... YOU KNOW AS WELL AS I DO THAT I'M NOT LEAVING THIS ROOM. SO LET'S BOTH GET USED TO IT.
DAMMIT... THERE'S SO MUCH I HAVEN'T TOLD YOU...

... SO MUCH TRUTH... YOU STILL DON'T KNOW...

240
PRIVATE

I'M NOT LOOKING FORWARD TO THIS CONVERSATION...

... PAUL'S A BIT OF AN ECCENTRIC, Y'KNOW.
UNDERSTATEMENT OF THE YEAR, I'D SAY. BUT EVEN HE NEEDS TO SEE THIS IS A LOST CAUSE.
LET'S JUST GET THIS OVER WITH.

... I WANT YOU BOTH TO KNOW, I'M PROTESTING THIS DECISION WITH ALL THE STRENGTH I CAN MUSTER.
TALK TO THE ADMINISTRATOR. I'M JUST RELAYING THE MESSAGE...

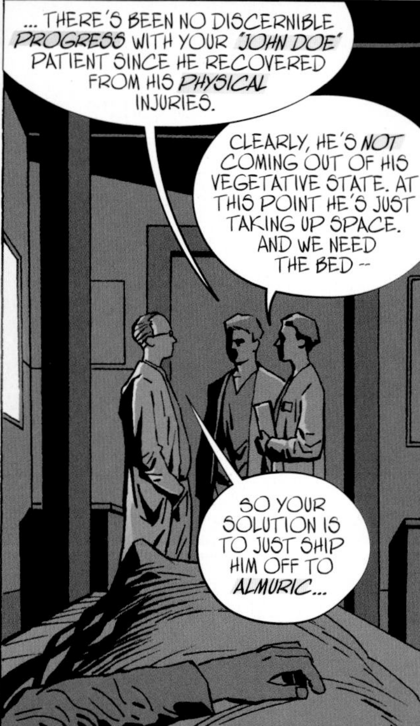
... THERE'S BEEN NO DISCERNIBLE PROGRESS WITH YOUR "JOHN DOE" PATIENT SINCE HE RECOVERED FROM HIS PHYSICAL INJURIES.
CLEARLY, HE'S NOT COMING OUT OF HIS VEGETATIVE STATE. AT THIS POINT HE'S JUST TAKING UP SPACE. AND WE NEED THE BED --
SO YOUR SOLUTION IS TO JUST SHIP HIM OFF TO ALMURIC...

... LOCK HIM AWAY WITH THE OTHER "CRAZIES" AND THROW AWAY THE KEY...?!
I'M TELLING YOU THERE'S STILL SOMEONE IN THERE. AND BELIEVE ME --

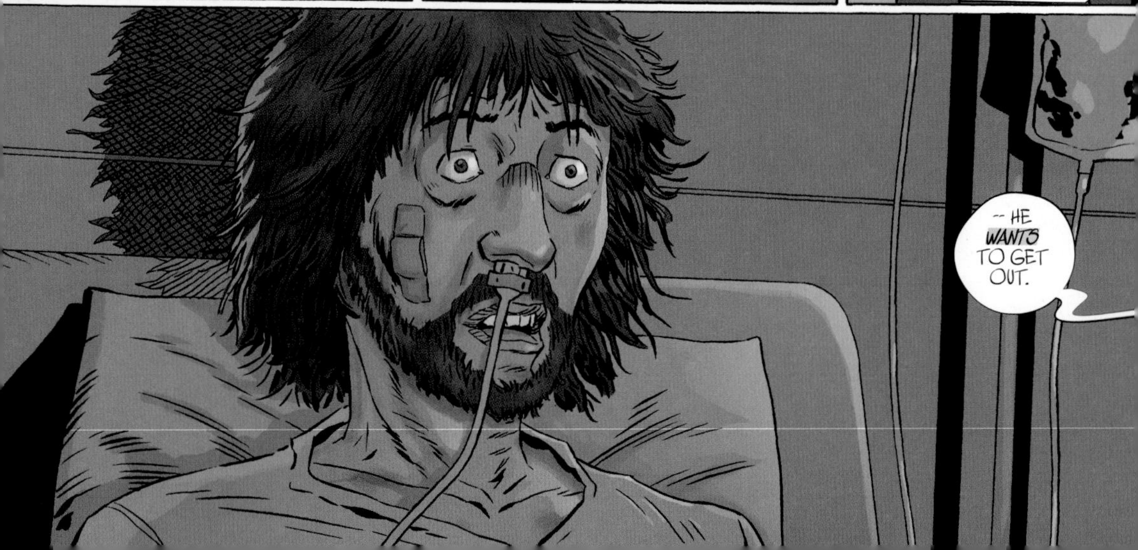
-- HE WANTS TO GET OUT.

SEX

CHAPTER THIRTY
ANOTHER POUND OF FLESH

JOE CASEY WRITER · PIOTR KOWALSKI ARTIST · BRAD SIMPSON COLORIST · RUS WOOTON LETTERER · SONIA HARRIS GRAPHIC DESIGNER

O MAYOR EDGWICK HOUGHT I OULD... WELL, OME SEE YOU IN PERSON...
I'M... UMMM... ASSUMING WE'RE ALONE...
... THAT THIS ROOM IS, Y'KNOW, SECURE --
YOU CAN STOP BEATING AROUND THE BUSH, TUCKER. LARRY'S AT THE OFFICE...

... AND YOUR LOVE LIFE MATTERS TO ME NOT IN THE LEAST.
I ASSUME YOU'RE HERE ABOUT THE WEBER MEETING...?
WELL, IN A WAY, YEAH.

I MEAN, SEDGWICK THOUGHT HE FACT THAT YOU'RE A LITTLE... INCAPACITATED AT THE MOMENT...
... ALTHOUGH, NO ONE TOLD ME EXACTLY WHAT HAPPENED TO YOU...
CUT MYSELF SHAVING.

OKAY. WELL... IN ANY EVENT, MISTER WEBER HAS BEEN MADE AWARE OF YOUR CURRENT CIRCUMSTANCES.
SO IF YOU WANT TO POSTPONE OR --
NO...

... WE'RE NOT POSTPONING ANYTHING.
THE MEETING IS ON.
IN FACT... I'M REALLY LOOKING FORWARD TO IT.

NO DOUBT YOU'RE WONDERING WHAT THE FUCK YOU'RE DOIN' HERE...

... THIS IS A MUTHAFUCKIN' CLEAN ROOM, BY THE WAY. NOTHING BUT US AND YOU.
SO YOU JUST KEEP YOUR PUSSY IN PARK, SISTER.
WE KNOW WHAT'S UP.

YOU'RE LUCKY WE FOUND YOU WHEN WE DID. OUR BOY TOLD US HE PICKED YOU UP WHILE YOU WERE ON THE RUN FROM THE COPS.
NOW... TIME TO TALK BUSINESS.

YOU CATCHIN' OUR DRIFT HERE? OR YOU FEELIN' LIKE MAKIN' SOME TROUBLE...?

... WHAT KIND OF TROUBLE COULD I POSSIBLY CAUSE?
I'M SOMEONE WHO JUST... I DUNNO... ACTS ON INSTINCT.
I KNOW I SHOULDN'T OPEN UP LIKE THIS TO YOU TWO. BUT I JUST CAN'T HELP MYSELF...

... Y'KNOW, I DON'T USUALLY DO THIS.

BUT I THINK WHEN PEOPLE ARE SOMEHOW... THRUST TOGETHER LIKE THIS, THEY SHOULD SEE IT AS AN OPPORTUNITY, DON'T YOU?
I MEAN... THE THREE OF US, COOPED UP IN HERE...

... I FEEL LIKE IT'S SOMETHING WE COULD DEFINITELY TAKE ADVANTAGE OF.
H-HOLD UP, NOW...
WE AIN'T HERE TO DANCE, GIRL...

WHO SAID ANYTHING ABOUT DANCING --
YOU GOT NO SHAME...

... THEN AGAIN, YOU ALWAYS WERE A WILD CARD, WEREN'T YOU?
EVEN THE OLD MAN NEVER THOUGHT TO BRING YOU IN FROM THE COLD. YOU'RE LIKE DYNAMITE.
HHNNT
NNNFF

IT'S POINTLESS TO FIGHT IT, FELLAS. THIS CONNECTION IS STRONG.
TELL ME YOU DON'T FEEL IT --
SAVE THE SEDUCTION RAP...

... IT AIN'T GONNA WORK THIS TIME.
UFF!

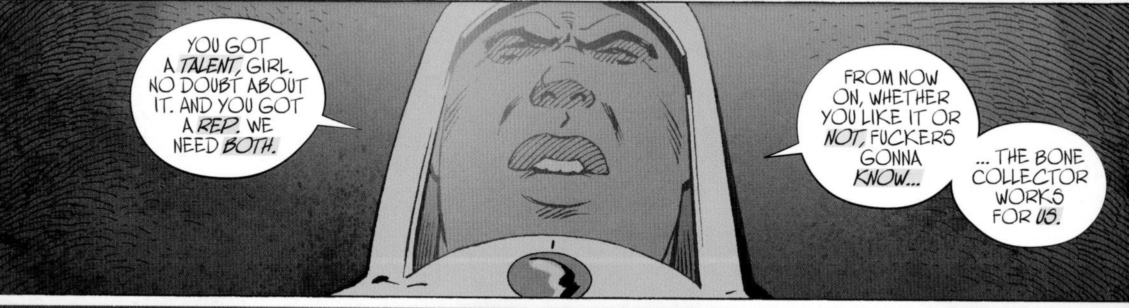
YOU GOT A TALENT, GIRL. NO DOUBT ABOUT IT. AND YOU GOT A REP. WE NEED BOTH.
FROM NOW ON, WHETHER YOU LIKE IT OR NOT, FUCKERS GONNA KNOW...
... THE BONE COLLECTOR WORKS FOR US.

THIS IS A FAR FUCKIN' CRY FROM WHAT YOU'RE KNOWN FOR, ALBERT...

... I MEAN, IT'S NOT EXACTLY HACKING A STATE-OF-THE-ART DATABASE, IS IT...?
DISH UZ THOMTING UH HAD THUPPED OVUH FUM URUP. UTZ UN AINSHENT DOME DUT PRE-DUHTS UVUHN DUH DIMUN SOOTRUH...

OKAY...
... SO IT'S OLDER THAN THE DIAMOND SUTRA. BIG DEAL. WHAT'S THAT GOT TO DO WITH THIS "VIZ IBN ZIYAD"?
UH DINK DUS NAM HUZ SUM DEEPUH MEEDING... SUM SUT UHF POWUHFUL ENDITY...
... SUM UHF ID CUN BUH FUND UN DUH DEXTS...
SAY WHAT...?!
THE NAME HAS A DEEPER MEANING. A POWERFUL ENTITY... SOMETHING HE FOUND IN THE TEXTS...

... SPEAKING OF WHICH, I DON'T EVEN KNOW WHAT LANGUAGE THIS THING IS WRITTEN IN.
IT'S NOTHING I'VE EVER SEEN BEFORE. LIKE SOME SORT OF WEIRD SANSKRIT-HIEROGLYPHIC COMBO...

YETH!
UT DOTHNT HUV UH NUM, DIS LUNGUGE...
ALBERT...

... YOU'RE GETTING A LITTLE TOO EXCITED HERE. AND IT'S STARTING TO PISS ME OFF.

SO IF THERE'S INFO IN THERE THAT WE CAN ACTUALLY USE, YOU'D BETTER COUGH IT UP QUICK.
YOU CATCHIN' MY DRIFT HERE, FUCKFACE?
YOU KNOW CHA CHA CAN BE A LITTLE IMPATIENT, DON'T YOU?
WELL, I'M NOT FAR BEHIND HIM. IF YOU CAN READ ANY OF THIS, GO AHEAD.
BUT TALK SLOWLY SO WE CAN UNDERSTAND YOU...
UHHHH, OHTAY...
"... EEDURNA UXISTUNZ US UNDULGED BUH UNLUH UN. HUH US HUSTRY'S HURTIK...
"... ETERNAL EXISTENCE IS INDULGED BY ONLY ONE. HE IS HISTORY'S HERETIC...
"HUH LUKS DUHN UPUH DUH WUHD UN PUHSUVS UTS VURUH UDGES...
"HE LOOKS DOWN UPON THE WORLD AND PERCEIVES ITS VERY EDGES...
... "UND HUH RUSHUPS DUH WUHD TUH SOOT HUZ NUHDS."
"... AND HE RESHAPES THE WORLD TO SUIT HIS NEEDS."
NOT TOO MESSIANIC, EH? SOUNDS LIKE A REAL MOTHERFUCKER.
MAYBE. BUT IF THE OLD MAN WAS WILLING TO DIG DEEPER...
... MAYBE WE SHOUL TOO.

SO THIS IS THE SUB-BASEMENT...?
THIS'LL WORK. YOU CAN GO NOW.
YES, SIR.

OKAY, SO...
... AM I ALONE IN HERE?

ABSOLUTELY NOT, SIMON.
I HAVE TO SAY... I ADMIRE YOUR STAMINA. YOU CERTAINLY DON'T LOOK SO GOOD.

YOU SHOULD SEE THE OTHER GUYS.
SO... CLEARLY MAYOR SEDGWICK THOUGHT IT WAS A GOOD IDEA FOR US TO HAVE A CONVERSATION. WHY, I HAVE NO IDEA.
WELL, I'D LIKE TO THINK YOU HAVE SOME IDEA. YOU'RE A SMART MAN. AS TO THE TYPE OF CONVERSATION WE SHOULD HAVE...
... I THINK THAT DEPENDS ENTIRELY ON YOU.

FIRST OF ALL, IS IT BAD FORM TO ADMIT THAT I'M INTERESTED IN THE STATUS OF THE KANSEI MERGER...?
POSSIBLY. BUT SINCE I DECIDED AGAINST IT, I'LL ALLOW IT.
IT WASN'T THE RIGHT FIT.
HONESTLY, I CAN'T TELL YOU HOW RELIEVED I AM TO HEAR THAT. IT ABSOLUTELY WASN'T THE RIGHT FIT.
NOW, MORE THAN EVER.
SO IS IT BAD FORM TO ASK WHY YOU'RE SO INTERESTED IN THE STATE OF MY COMPANY?
FIRST OF ALL, IT'S NOT SO MUCH YOUR COMPANY I'M INTERESTED IN SIMON.
IT'S YOU.

ECOND OF
LL, I DON'T
NK ANYONE'S
N YOU THE KIND
CREDIT YOU
DESERVE.
WHEN WE FIRST MET AT THE AMBASSADOR HOTEL, I TRIED TO PLAY IT COOL. I'M SURE YOU THOUGHT... WELL, I DON'T KNOW WHAT YOUR IMPRESSION OF ME WAS THAT NIGHT...
BUT I'M NOT GOING TO BE NEARLY AS COY TONIGHT. I HAVE A QUESTION I'D LIKE TO ASK YOU...
... DO YOU THINK THE WORLD IS WORKING?

WAS THAT TOO ESOTERIC OF A QUESTION...?
DEPENDS ON WHAT YOU'RE REFERRING TO.

I'LL BE MORE DIRECT: DOES THE WORLD -- AS IT IS -- MAKE SENSE TO YOU?
AT THE MOMENT, THIS MEETING ISN'T MAKING A LOT OF SENSE TO ME.
JUST WHO ARE YOU REPRESENTING, MISTER WEBER...?
LET'S SAY I'M HERE ON BEHALF OF PEOPLE WHO HAVE A VESTED INTEREST IN THE WORLD MAKING SENSE...
... CERTAINLY MUCH BETTER SENSE THAN IT DOES RIGHT NOW.

SOUNDS LIKE A... WORTHWHILE ENDEAVOR.
ALTHOUGH... I GUESS IT ALL DEPENDS ON HOW ONE DEFINES THE *IDEA* OF THE WORLD "MAKING SENSE".
VERY GOOD. WE ADMIRE A HEALTHY SKEPTICISM.
REST ASSURED... YOU *WANT* TO KNOW HOW THE PEOPLE I REPRESENT DEFINE THAT IDEA. THAT'S THE MAIN REASON I'M HERE... TO OPEN A *DIALOGUE*.
I CAN SPEA FROM PERSO EXPERIENC THIS IS THE S YOU *WANT* T BE ON...
... SO, BY ALL MEANS, CONSIDER WHAT I'VE SAID. AND LET'S TALK AGAIN VERY SOON.
IN THE MEANTIME... FEEL BETTER.

THIS IS WEBER REPORTING IN.
FIRST THINGS FIRST. THE KANSEI DEAL IS DEAD.

HE DID IT HIMSELF... WHICH I TAKE AS A VERY GOOD SIGN THAT HIS GOALS CAN INDEED ALIGN WITH OURS.
MAY I SAY SOMETHING? YOU DIDN'T SEE THE STATE HE WAS IN... AND THE FACT THAT EVEN I COULDN'T SUSS OUT HOW HE GOT THAT WAY SAYS VOLUMES ABOUT HOW DISCREETLY HE CONDUCTS HIS LIFE.
OUT OF ALL THE CANDIDATES I'VE PROPOSED TO THE STEERING COMMITTEE, MUCH LESS THE CHAIRMAN...

...I'VE NEVER BEEN MORE CERTAIN. SIMON COOKE BELONGS WITH US.

THE TIMING IS PERFECT. OUR UPCOMING MEETING IS EXACTLY WHAT HE NEEDS TO EXPERIENCE TO UNDERSTAND WHAT WE'RE DOING HERE.

SO LET'S TALK ABOUT THE NEXT STEP. LET'S TALK ABOUT HOW TO GET HIM THERE...

... YOU EVER *BEEN* TO ALMURIC HOSPITAL?
ARE YOU SERIOUS? WHY WOULD I EVER WANT TO SET FOOT IN *THAT* HELLHOLE?!
INTENSIVE CARE
I'M A SURGEON, NOT A SHRINK.
OKAY, OKAY... FAIR ENOUGH. BUT I'VE BEEN THINKING ABOUT WHAT *DOCTOR PAUL* SAID ABOUT SHIPPING HIS PATIENT THERE.
NOT THAT I'D SAY THIS TO THE ADMINISTRATOR I DON'T WANT TO COME ACROSS AS SOME SORT OF --
-- BLEEDING HEART...
OH MY GOD...!

JEEZUS... J-JOHN DOE... HE...
C-CALL SECURITY...!

PANT!
PANT!
PANT!

HUH--!
THERE HE IS--!

ROOFTOP ACCESS

GUUHHNNT--!

SO THIS IS WHAT IT HAS COME TO. HOW PATHETIC...
... DID THE EVOLUTION ENGINEERE COUNT FO NOTHING?

OUR MASTER IS EXTREMELY DISPLEASED.
H-HOLY SHIT...
... MAGHAZO...!
WE SENT YOU HERE EMPOWERED. WE SENT YOU HERE WITH PURPOSE...

... YOU ARE NOT THE BRINGER OF CHAOS WE FASHIONED YOU TO BE.
WH- WHU....
B-BU PURP
... RETIRE

NONSENSE. I CAN FEEL YOUR RESISTANCE.
ONCE AGAIN, YOU HAVE BEEN TOO DEEPLY INFECTED BY TH SINS OF THE FLES BUT, AS ALWAYS, THAT FLESH BETRA A ROTTED CARCASS.
AND NOW... A NEW PURITY MUST BE ACHIEVED.

OU MUST DISCOVER LL THAT OU HAVE LOST.
NO...
OUR MASTER CALLS TO YOU. HE HONORS YOU BY SPEAKING YOUR NAME.
YOU WILL ANSWER THAT CALL...

... IT IS YOUR DESTINY.
GYE EAAAAA--

HAT THE ELL WAS THAT--?!
HAD TO BE HIM.
EVERYONE -- POSITIONS! NOW... ONE... TWO --

-- THREE!

WHAT THE FUCK--?!
WHERE THE HELL DID HE GO...?!

HEY, IT'S TUCKER. JUST WANTED TO... I DUNNO... CHECK IN. BEEN AWHILE SINCE WE TALKED... OR ANYTHING...
... LOOK, I KNOW IT GOT WEIRD. I DUNNO WHAT ELSE I CAN SAY TO CONVINCE YOU TO --
BEEP
... I KNOW IT'S AFTER HOURS, BUT I FIGURED THIS MIGHT BE THE BEST TIME TO TALK...
... Y'KNOW, ABOUT SIMON. I HEARD HE'S LEFT THE HOSPITAL...
OKAY, WARREN... STRAIGHT UP. I ALWAYS KNEW ABOUT HIM. AND I FIGURED THAT, AS HIS LAWYER, YOU WERE ALWAYS COVERING FOR HIM WHENEVER IT WAS NECESSARY.
YOU'RE LUCKY I VALUE LOYALTY AS MUCH I DO.
ABOUT HIM... WELL, I'M NOT SURE HOW I FEEL AT THIS POINT. I WARNED HIM AGAINST THIS KIND OF BACKSLIDING --
ACTUALLY, I'VE BEEN THINKING... IF I'M BEING OPEN WITH YOU TWO ABOUT WHAT I KNOW...
... THEN IT'S TIME YOU TWO BRING ME COMPLETELY INSIDE. THERE ARE STILL THINGS ABOUT THIS COMPANY THAT AREN'T EXACTLY NORMAL...

ARE YOU SURE YOU WANT TO BE ALONE, MISTER COOKE...?
I'LL BE FINE FOR THE NIGHT. YOU CAN CHECK IN ON ME IN THE MORNING...

I TAKE IT THIS IS THE RESULT OF YOUR ONGOING IDENTITY CRISIS. NOT EXACTLY LIKE RIDING A BIKE, IS IT...?
I DID FINE... CONSIDERING I WAS COMPLETELY UNPROTECTED.
WHAT CAN I DO FOR YOU, ANNABELLE...?
FOR ME? NOTHING. BUT YOU WANTED ME TO SPY ON YOUR STALKER, DIDN'T YOU?
HIS GUYS WERE ONLY MARGINALLY SECURITY CONSCIOUS. BUT I STILL WENT OLD SCHOOL.
A SIMPLE SURVEILLANCE BUG ATTACHED TO THEIR WHEEL WELL... NEVER UNDERESTIMATE THE POWER OF A LOW-LEVEL RADIO FREQUENCY. JUST A STEP ABOVE CITIZENS BAND.

AS USUAL, YOU'RE ON THE CUTTING EDGE, ANNABELLE.
LINEAR THINKING. YOU SHOULD TRY IT SOMETIME.
ANYWAY, I GLEANED QUITE A BIT FROM LISTENING IN ON HIS PHONE CALLS. IT SEEMS YOUR NEW BOYFRIEND, WEBER...

... HE'S PART OF THE ROTHCHILD GROUP.
DAMN...
... OF COURS
I WASN'T SURE THEY ACTUALLY EXISTED. YOU KNOW ME... I'M NOT BIG ON ILLUMINATI CONSPIRACIES. BUT HE WAS CERTAINLY TALKING LIKE THEY WERE LEGIT.
I'M BETTING THEY WERE NEVER PART OF YOUR ROGUES' GALLERY...

WHY WOULD THEY BE? I CERTAINLY WOULDN'T CLASSIFY THEM AS CRIMINALS. WHAT THEY PURPORT TO DO... AT LEAST FROM THE RUMORS I'VE HEARD... IT'S NOT EXACTLY IN MY WHEELHOUSE. NOT ON EITHER SIDE OF MY OLD DOUBLE-LIFE.
WELL, WEBER'S SPEECH MAKES COMPLETE SENSE TO ME NOW. NOT TO MENTION, WHY HE WAS SO CAGEY.
I CAN'T BELIEVE I DIDN'T SUSS THIS OUT ON MY OWN...!

I REALLY AM SLIPPING --
OKAY, LISTEN... THERE'S SOMETHING ELSE YOU SHOULD BE MADE AWARE OF. SOMETHING A LITTLE MORE PERSONAL.
I DON'T ENJOY BE THE ONE TO OPEN WOUNDS.

... BUT IT'S ABOUT KEENAN WADE.
I THINK YOUR FORMER SIDEKICK IS IN SOME DEEP SHIT.

SEX

CHAPTER THIRTY-ONE
DISAPPEARING INK

JOE CASEY WRITER · PIOTR KOWALSKI ARTIST · BRAD SIMPSON COLORIST · RUS WOOTON LETTERER · SONIA HARRIS GRAPHIC DESIGNER

SATURN CITY:
SO HOW FREAKED OUT ARE YOU...?
I DUNNO, KEENAN...
... I MEAN, SIMON COOKE?! IN A MILLION YEARS, I NEVER WOULDA THOUGHT...!
WELL, YOU'RE ON THE INSIDE NOW, BABY.
AS FAR AS I KNOW, THERE WERE MAYBE THREE OR FOUR PEOPLE IN THE WORLD WHO KNEW THAT SECRET. NOW THERE'S ONE MORE...
... YOU.
Pelican • Tour

SO, THIS "QUINN" WOMAN... SHE REALLY THOUGHT YOU WERE HOT SHIT, HUH...?
WELL, IT WAS A CERTAIN KIND OF GAME WE WERE PLAYING, Y'KNOW. A CERTAIN KIND OF... SUBTEXT INVOLVED, I GUESS.
WHAT AM I SAYING? YOU READ IT...
... IT WAS ALL RIGHT THERE, WASN'T IT?
In hindsight, I suppose things were doomed from the start...

... and no matter what I did, I couldn't facilitate a healthy working relationship.
Simon simply wasn't interested... and Keenan wasn't going to take any shit when he was more than capable of doing what was required...

To say the least.

At that point, there was nothing I could do but watch it all fall apart.

I hated seeing Keenan go. So much talent. So much potential.
But I didn't have any real reason to stop him...

... seeing as I'd already received word of my own diagnosis.

SHE NEVER TOLD ME ABOUT THE CANCER THAT WAS KILLING HER.
I WOULD'VE LIKED TO HAVE KNOWN.

SO, LISTEN... I DUNNO WHAT IT ALL ADDS UP TO. BUT IT DEFINITELY PUTS THIS THING WITH THE BREAKS INTO SOME SORT OF PERSPECTIVE.
SIMON QUIT. THAT'S HIS CROSS TO BEAR.
ME? I KNOW THERE'S STILL SHIT THAT NEEDS TO BE DONE --
OKAY...

... HOLD ON A SECOND.
I MAY STILL BE ABSORBING ALL THIS, BUT ONE THING I DO KNOW... IS THAT I DIDN'T NEED TO READ SOME OLD LADY'S MEMOIR TO BE CONVINCED OF ANYTHING WHEN IT COMES TO YOU.
WHAT DO YOU MEAN...?

IT'S NO SECRET TO ME THAT YOU'RE SPECIAL. I KNOW THIS CITY AND WHAT LIVING HERE MEANS.
I KNOW YOU'VE GOT THINGS YOU'VE GOTTA DO TO TRY AND MAKE IT BETTER FOR THE REST OF US.
SO I'M WITH YOU, BABY. NO MATTER WHAT...

... I HOPE YOU GET THAT.
I DO GET IT...

... AND I DON'T TAKE IT FOR GRANTED, EITHER. IT'S WHY I'VE TOLD YOU EVERYTHING.

I LOVE YOU, VERNITA.
YOU'D BETTER, WISEASS.

THE NEW CHAPTER
STAY FIT
NIGHT CLUB
THE HOUSE OF FIRE
DINER

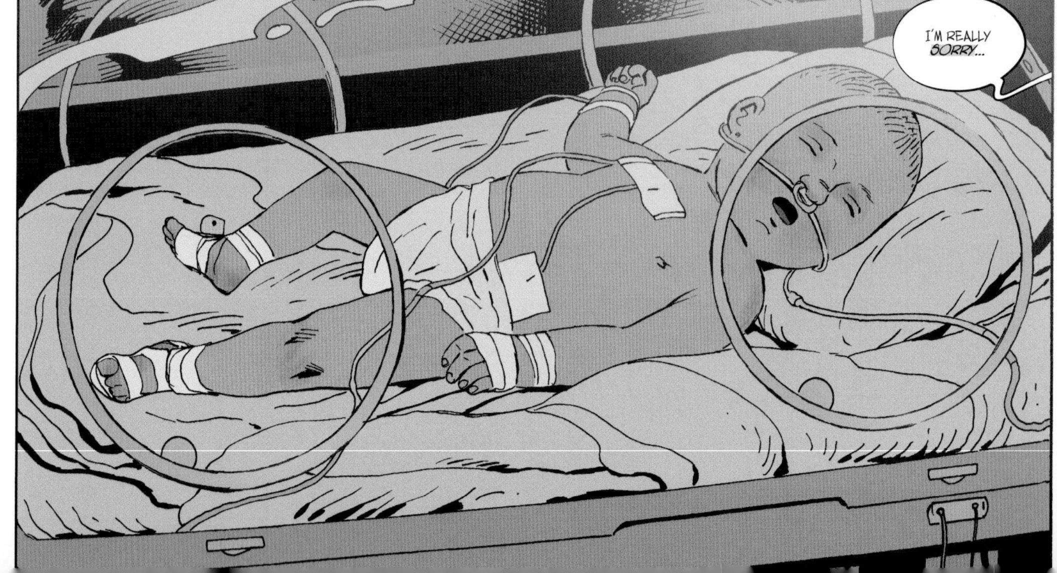
I'M REALLY SORRY...

... I JUST DON'T KNOW... WHAT TO *DO* WITH YOU...
I C-CAN'T... I JUST *CAN'T*...

... SO THE *KID'S* GETTIN' HEALTHIER EVERY DAY. BUT *SHEILA'S*... WELL, SHE'S FREAKIN' ME OUT...
YOU DON'T SAY.
ST. MARX HOSPITAL; MATERNITY WARD:

WELL, SHE *DID* JUST GIVE BIRTH. HER BABY ALMOST *DIED*. WHAT DO YOU *EXPECT?*
SHE'S BEEN THROUGH A *LOT*.
NAH, I'M *TELLIN'* YOU, MISS LAGRAVENESE... SHE AIN'T *ACTING* RIGHT.

IT'S *MORE* THAN JUST *MEDICAL* SHIT.
YOU'LL SEE.

SHEILA...

... I HEAR THERE'S GOOD NEWS ON THE RECOVERY FRONT WHERE YOUR OFFSPRING'S CONCERNED.
OH, C'MON. WHAT'RE YOU DOIN' DOWN ON THE FLOOR, GIRL...?
HAVE YOU... Y'KNOW... GONE IN AND, I DUNNO, HELD THE KID YET?
KID NEEDS HIS MOMMA...

HEY, SHEILA. LOOK AT ME.
I SYMPATHIZE, OKAY? YOU DIDN'T SIGN UP FOR THIS... YOU'RE IN A LITTLE OVER YOUR HEAD.
BUT EVERYTHING SEEMS TO BE TURNING OUT ALRIGHT...

HMMF.
OKAY.
WELL, LISTEN... WE'RE HERE TO TRY AND HELP YOU...

... JUST AS SOON AS WE CAN FIGURE OUT HOW.
RIGHT, SKYSCRAPER...?
UHHH... YEAH...

SHE'S BEEN IN THERE FOR ABOUT AN HOUR NOW...
... STILL HAVEN'T SEEN OR HEARD JACK SHIT.
JUST AS LONG AS YOU FUKKAS GOT ALL THE EXITS COVERED --

-- THIS IS WHERE SHE SHOWS US HOW MUCH DAMAGE SHE'S REALLY CAPABLE OF, Y'DIG?
SHE SEEMED INTO IT, RAY. I'M TELLIN' YOU --
HOLD ON... SHE'S COMIN' BACK...

DON'T TAKE NOTHIN' FOR GRANTED, SOLLY. SHE'S ONE CONNIVING PIECE O' PUSSY...
TREAT HER ASS LIKE NITROGLYCERIN --
NO SWEAT. MY BOYS GOT IT COVERED...

THERE YOU ARE. NICE AND SLOW, BITCH.
ONE FALSE MOVE AND YOU'RE A STAIN ON THE ASPHALT...
NO NEED TO BULLY ME, GUYS --

-- I DID EXACTLY WHAT I WAS ASKED TO DO.
WHOEVER RUNS THE CREW THAT HANGS OUT IN THIS DIVE WILL JUST HAVE TO DEAL WITH BEING A CREW SHORT.
DON'T WORRY. THEY LOVED IT...

OOOHHH YESSSSS--!
HHHNNNGGGG!

YES-YES-YES-YES-YES...!
AAAAOOOWWWW!

WHEW!
ONE OF THE FEW PERKS OF HAVING HISTORY, I GUESS...
... AT LEAST YOU HAVE EXPERIENCE TO DRAW ON. YOU ALWAYS KNEW EXACTLY WHERE TO PUT YOUR MOUTH ON ME.
THAT... REALLY TOOK MY MIND OFF THIS DEAD END STORY...
WELL, JULIETTE, MY DEAR, IF THAT'S WHAT IT TAKES --

-- YOU KNOW I'M NOT ABOVE HE OCCASIONAL BOOTY CALL FROM AN EX-WIFE.
YOUR STORY'S GOING THAT BADLY, HUH...?
THAT'S AN UNDERSTATEMENT, BORIS. ANYONE WORTH TALKING TO DOESN'T WANT TO TALK TO ME.

YOU'RE JUST USED TO PLAYING BY THE RULES, THAT'S ALL. UNLIKE ME, YOU'VE GOT RESPECTABILITY.
SPEAKING OF WHICH, I HEARD A RUMOR ABOUT YOUR BOY, SIMON...

... HE JUST GOT OUT FROM A BRIEF HOSPITAL STAY.
THE HOSPITAL? WHAT FOR...?

THAT, I DON'T KNOW. BUT IT WAS ALL KEPT PRETTY HUSH-HUSH.
ONE OF MY AMBULANCE-CHASER PALS HEARD SOME CHATTER DOWN AT ST. MARX. WE WERE THINKING ABOUT RUNNING A STORY OURSELVES, BUT WE DIDN'T HAVE ENOUGH TO GO ON...
SINCE WHEN HAS THAT EVER STOPPED YOU...?

HEY, NOW... TABLOID JOURNALISM HAS ITS OWN BRAND OF ETHICS. BESIDES, WE'RE IN A PHASE WHERE WE'RE TRYING TO AVOID LAWSUITS.
I'M SURE THAT WON'T LAST --
OKAY, I KNOW THIS IS STARTING TO GET A LITTLE UNHEALTHY.
BUT I TRUST MY INSTINCTS AND EVERY TIME I HIT SOME DEAD END, I STILL THINK I'M ONTO SOMETHING...
THERE'S SOMETHING ABOUT SIMON COOKE THAT'S NOT ADDING UP.
HE'S DEFINITELY HIDING SOMETHING...
... I JUST HAVE NO IDEA WHAT.
JEEZUS CHRIST...
BOYS AND THEIR FUCKING TOYS...
YOU SAY SOMETHING, LARRY...?
JUST THAT... OH, NEVER MIND.
THANKS FOR THE INVITE.
THE THIRTEENTH FLOO

SO... THE ROTHCHILD GROUP...
... THIS IS JUST ONE OF THOSE THINGS I NEVER PAID ATTENTION TO BEFORE. MAYBE ON PURPOSE.
I DON'T BLAME YOU. BUT WE'RE IN IT NOW...

... THIS WEBER CHARACTER THINKS I'M A PRIME CANDIDATE FOR MEMBERSHIP. AND HE'S TENACIOUS.
PERSONALLY, I DON'T SEE IT. I NEVER PEGGED YOU AS THE PUPPET MASTER TYPE...

T THE "ROTHCHILDREN" Y THE LONG GAME. BY ACCOUNTS, THEY'RE WORKING TOWARD ESTABLISHING A ONE-WORLD GOVERNMENT.
IF HANGING OUT WITH ELITIST INTELLECTUALS IN SECRET MEETINGS AROUND THE GLOBE ACTUALLY INTERESTS YOU...
STOP IT. WE'RE TALKING ABOUT A POSSIBLE CENTURY'S WORTH OF BEHIND-THE-SCENES POLITICAL MANEUVERING AND SOCIOLOGICAL MANIPULATION...!

YOU MEAN, THE SORT OF CRIMES THAT AREN'T BY-THE-BOOK ILLEGAL...?
MAYBE I'M TOO APATHETIC TO BE A CONSPIRACY NUT.
I'D SAY THAT'S EXTREMELY LIKELY, WARREN...

... BUT THAT OESN'T MEAN IT'S NOT HAPPENING.
A SHADOWY CABAL OF POLITICAL LEADERS, CORPORATE HEADS, BONA FIDE ROYALS AND OTHER GLOBAL LUMINARIES THAT GET TOGETHER IN SECRET AND ACTUALLY SHAPE WORLD EVENTS? I DUNNO. THAT'S SCARY STUFF...
OKAY, FINE. SO THEY EXIST. BUT TO WHAT END...?

WHAT DOES ANYONE WITH THEIR IDEOLOGY REALLY WANT?
POWER.

FORGET ABOUT ANY "NEW WORLD ORDER" RHETORIC. THAT'S ALL IT IS... RHETORIC. IN REALITY, IT DOESN'T MEAN ANYTHING.
WHATEVER THEIR "GOALS" ARE... JUST THE WAY THEY OPERATE IS SUSPECT.
SO, YEAH. THIS MIGHT ACTUALLY BE... AN OPPORTUNITY.
UMMM... WHAT DO YOU MEAN BY THAT...?
WELL, MAYBE I SHOULD PURSUE THIS... FIND OUT WHAT IT'S ALL ABOUT...
AFTER ALL, THE BEST WAY TO EFFECTIVELY DISMANTLE SOMETHING...
... IS FROM WITHIN.

WHAT... ARE YOU SUGGESTING? SOME SORT OF STING OPERATION...?
I GUESS THAT DEPENDS...
... FIRST THINGS FIRST. I NEED TO FIND OUT EXACTLY WHAT WE'RE DEALING WITH HERE.
I KNOW YOU BOTH SEE ME FROM A CERTAIN PERSEPCTIVE. CONSIDERING MY RECENT BEHAVIOR, I GET IT.
BUT IF WE'RE TO ASSUME THE WORST ABOUT THE ROTHCHILD GROUP -- AND IF WE FIND OUT WE'RE RIGHT -- THEN SOMETHING'S GOT TO BE DONE. AND MAKE NO MISTAKE...
... THIS IS WHAT I DO.
OH DAMN.
SORRY TO SKEWER TH DRAMATIC MOMENT, BU I'M LATE...

A DRINK OVER ON MERCER.
IF IT'S OKAY WITH YOU, BOSS...
GO ON. IT'S FINE.

HOLED UP HERE IN THE MAN CAVE.
WHO, ME?

I'D LIKE TO THINK THE FATE OF THE FREE WORLD COULD STAND A FEW MORE ROUNDS OF THOUGHTFUL DISCUSSION...
... GOD WILLING.

HUH.
HER BALLS ARE GETTING BIGGER, AREN'T THEY...?
THE BIGGER, THE BETTER, AS FAR AS I'M CONCERNED.

IF YOU SAY SO. I'M JUST NOT SURE THAT THIS WON'T PUT YOUR BALLS ON THE CHOPPING BLOCK...
... WE BOTH KNOW THIS ON A MUCH HIGHER LEVEL THAN LOCAL STREET CRIME.

NOT TO MENTION THE FACT THAT YOU'RE SUPPOSED TO BE RETIRED --
SOMETHING I DIDN'T TELL LARRY...
... I'VE BEEN WORKING WITH ANNABELLE LAGRAVENESE ON THIS. SHE WAS THE ONE WHO FINALLY GOT THE INTEL.

OH JEEZUS... SIMON...
... YOU CAN'T JUST STAY AWAY FROM HER, CAN YOU...?
BELIEVE IT OR NOT, IT WAS STRICTLY PROFESSIONAL. SHE DID RIGHT BY ME.
THIS TIME, ANYWAY.

SOMETHING ELSE SHE TOLD ME, THOUGH... I'M NOT SURE HOW I FEEL ABOUT IT. OR HOW I SHOULD RESPOND.
SHE TOLD ME SHE'D RUN INTO KEENAN WADE...

... APPARENTLY, HE'S JOINED UP WITH THE BREAKS.
THE STREET GANG? NO FUCKING WAY...!
I ALWAYS THOUGHT KEENAN WAS A GOOD KID. WHAT IS HE THINKING...?!

I HAVE NO IDEA.
BUT I'M PRETTY SURE I NEED TO FIND OUT.

MERCER STREET:
P
ZONE

YOU'RE A PATHETIC PIECE OF SHIT, AREN'T YOU?!
YOU COULDN'T GET IT UP IF YOU HAD A GUN TO YOUR HEAD!

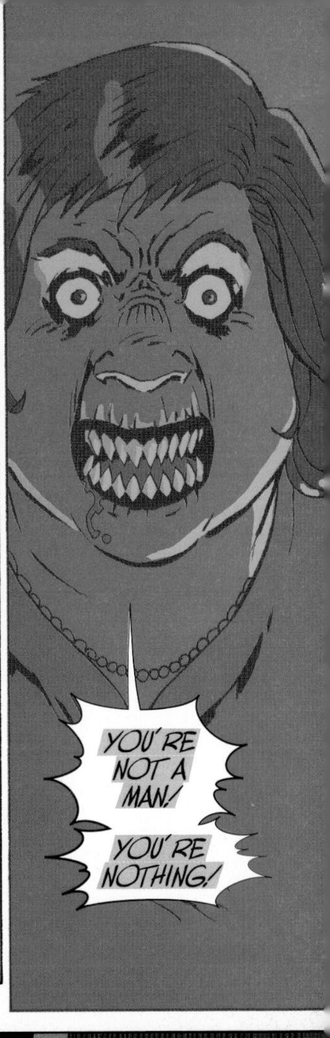
YOU'RE NOT A MAN!
YOU'RE NOTHING!

THERE YOU ARE, ELLIOT --

-- SORRY I'M A LITTLE LATE. TYPICAL COOKE COMPANY DRAMA.
WHAT'RE YOU DRINKING, THEN...?
WHATEVER IT TAKES, LORRAINE...

... SO WHAT EXACTLY CAN I DO FOR YOU?

WELL, FOR STARTERS... YOU CAN COME BACK TO WORK.
ARE YOU SERIOUS? LOOK AT ME. DO I LOOK LIKE A CAPABLE CORPORATE OFFICER TO YOU?

I KNOW YOU'RE BEEN DEALING WITH SOME... PERSONAL ISSUES. I GET IT. BUT I WANTED TO MEET WITH YOU FACE-TO-FACE TO TELL YOU WE NEED YOU.
I KNOW YOU DON'T KNOW ABOUT THIS...

... BUT SIMON IS JUST HOME FROM THE HOSPITAL.
HE IS...?
NOTHING SERIOUS, I HOPE. IS HE ALRIGHT...?

HE'S... GETTING THERE. BUT HE'S NOT A HUNDRED PERCENT YET. THAT'S WHY I NEED YOU IN THE OFFICE AGAIN. I NEED SOMEONE I CAN TRUST.
AFTER ALL, IT WASN'T LONG AGO THAT IT WAS PRETTY MUCH YOU AND I RUNNING THE WHOLE SHOW...

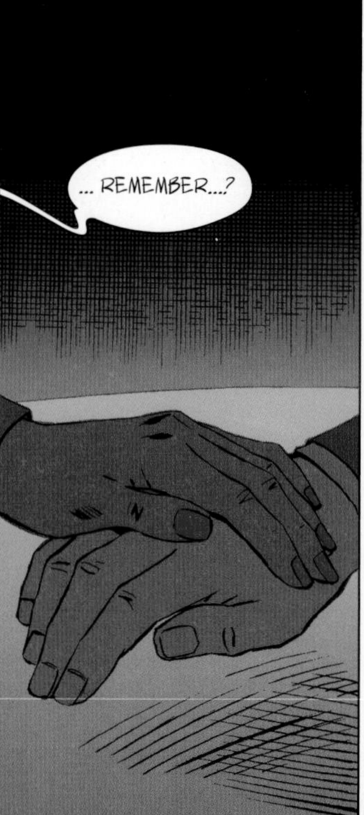
... REMEMBER...?

I REMEMBER.

Bar
I'M HEARING THINGS, Y'KNOW...

WINTERLANDS (SKINS' TERRITORY):

... THE BREAKS ARE MAKIN' MOVES. AND WHAT'RE WE DOING?
JUST WAITING FOR THEM TO SOLDIER RIGHT INTO OUR TERRITORY AND TAKE OVER? FUCK THAT.
YOU DRUNK MOTHERFUCKER. YOU GONNA CONVINCE BULLCHUCK OF THAT?! HE SAYS HE'S ALREADY GOT SOMETHING COOKING, BUT I DUNNO...

LISTEN... HE'S ALWAYS SAYIN' SHIT LIKE THAT. BUT SOMEONE'S GOTTA STEP UP AND LET THE BREAKS KNOW WE AIN'T ROLLIN' OVER.
A PREEMPTIVE STRIKE... AWWW YEAH...

I HEARD THAT FUCKHEAD, MASAI, IS DOIN' SOME REORGANIZING. GOT SOME NEW LIEUTENANTS HE'S GROOMING.
TARGET ONE A' THEM. THAT'LL SEND A MESSAGE, WON'T IT?
RIGHT... RIGHT... THAT'S SOME OLD SCHOOL SHIT THERE...

IT'D TAKE A VISIONARY ON OUR SIDE TO DO IT. THAT AIN'T ANY OF US, FELLAS. WE'RE JUST LOW-LEVEL GRUNTS.
NO SHIT. BUT THERE'S GOTTA BE SOMEONE IN THE RANKS WHO'D PUT IT ALL ON THE LINE. WHOEVER THAT BADASS IS COULD JUST TAKE OVER...

... HELL, I'D FOLLOW HIM.

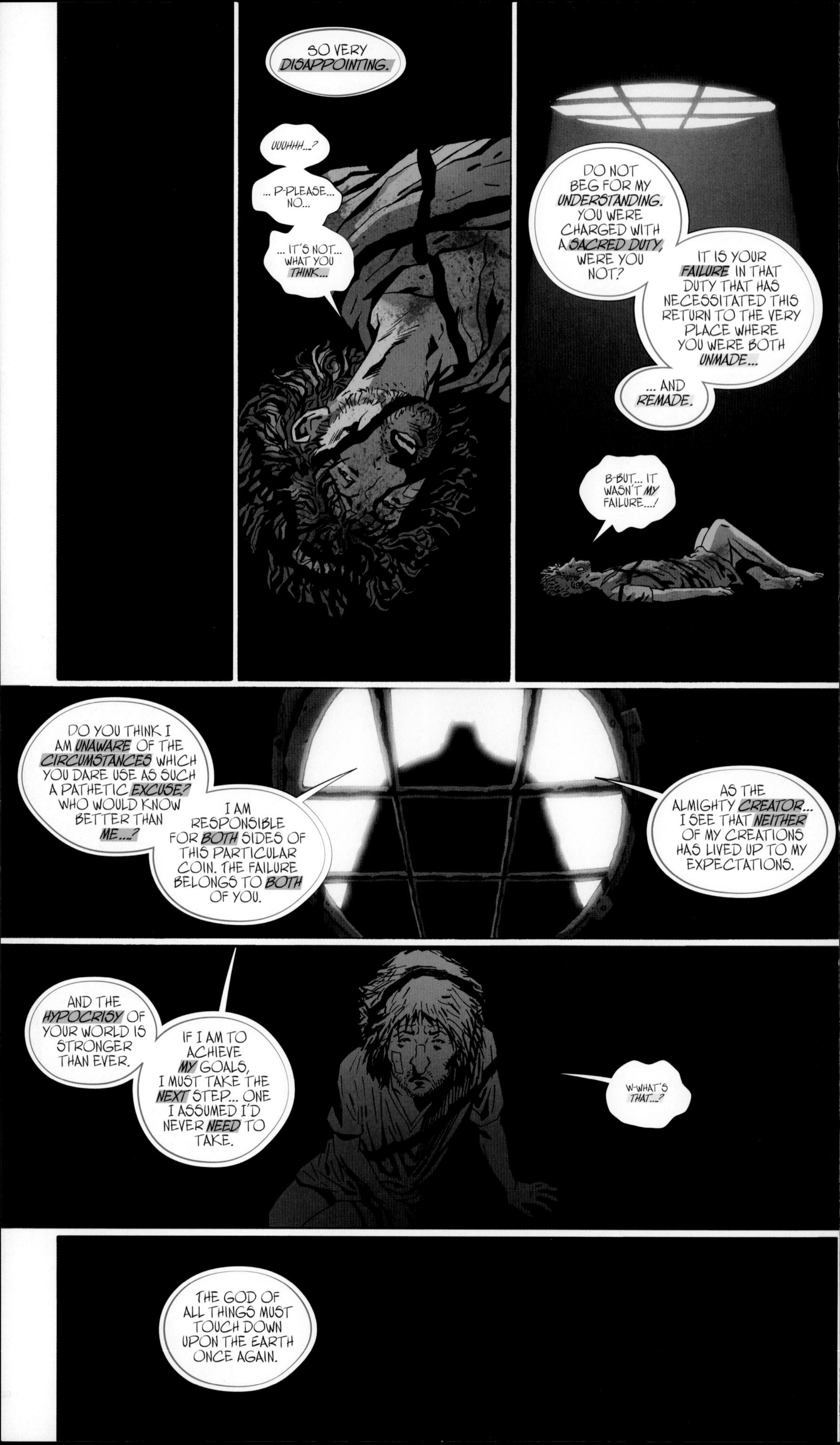
SO VERY DISAPPOINTING.
UUUHHH...?
... P-PLEASE... NO...
... IT'S NOT... WHAT YOU THINK...
DO NOT BEG FOR MY UNDERSTANDING. YOU WERE CHARGED WITH A SACRED DUTY, WERE YOU NOT?
IT IS YOUR FAILURE IN THAT DUTY THAT HAS NECESSITATED THIS RETURN TO THE VERY PLACE WHERE YOU WERE BOTH UNMADE...
... AND REMADE.
B-BUT... IT WASN'T MY FAILURE...!
DO YOU THINK I AM UNAWARE OF THE CIRCUMSTANCES WHICH YOU DARE USE AS SUCH A PATHETIC EXCUSE? WHO WOULD KNOW BETTER THAN ME...?
I AM RESPONSIBLE FOR BOTH SIDES OF THIS PARTICULAR COIN. THE FAILURE BELONGS TO BOTH OF YOU.
AS THE ALMIGHTY CREATOR... I SEE THAT NEITHER OF MY CREATIONS HAS LIVED UP TO MY EXPECTATIONS.
AND THE HYPOCRISY OF YOUR WORLD IS STRONGER THAN EVER.
IF I AM TO ACHIEVE MY GOALS, I MUST TAKE THE NEXT STEP... ONE I ASSUMED I'D NEVER NEED TO TAKE.
W-WHAT'S THAT...?
THE GOD OF ALL THINGS MUST TOUCH DOWN UPON THE EARTH ONCE AGAIN.

SEX™

CHAPTER THIRTY-TWO
LIVE IN SKIN

JOE CASEY WRITER · PIOTR KOWALSK
ARTIST · BRAD SIMPSON COLORIST
· RUS WOOTON LETTERER · SONIA
HARRIS GRAPHIC DESIGNER

THIS WAS RAFE RUSKO. HELLUVA LADIES' MAN...

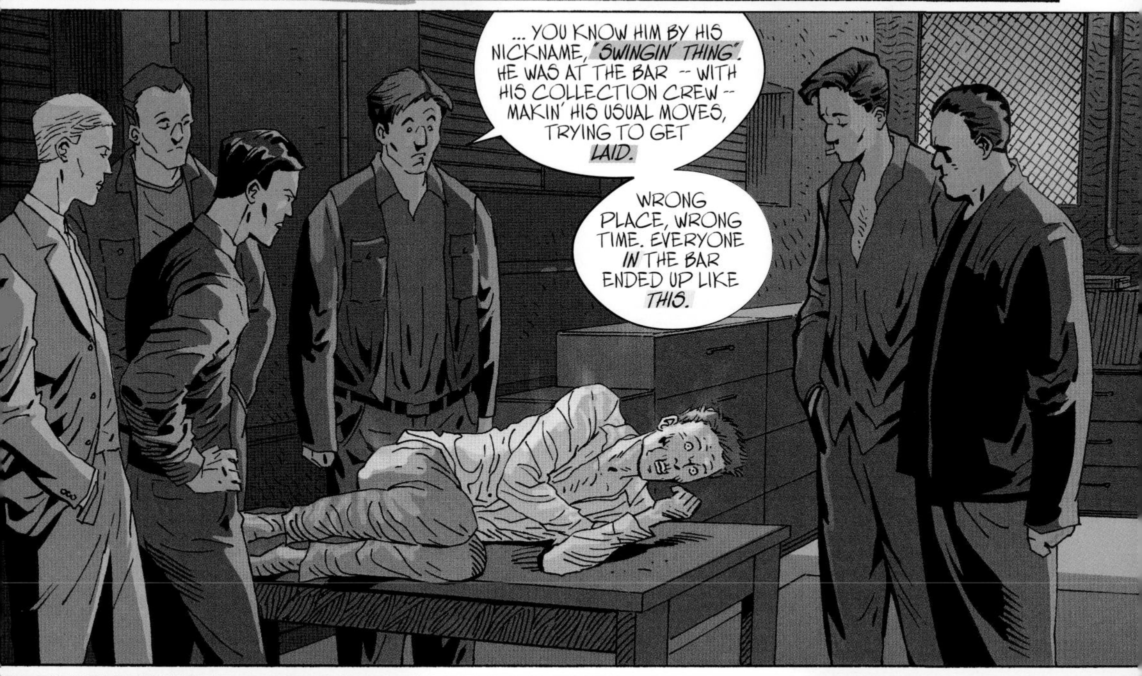
... YOU KNOW HIM BY HIS NICKNAME, 'SWINGIN' THING'. HE WAS AT THE BAR -- WITH HIS COLLECTION CREW -- MAKIN' HIS USUAL MOVES, TRYING TO GET LAID.
WRONG PLACE, WRONG TIME. EVERYONE IN THE BAR ENDED UP LIKE THIS.

SO... YOU DON'T THINK THIS WAS A RANDOM ACT, DO YOU, DOLPH...?
INDEED I DON'T. THIS WAS DELIBERATE.

DAMN RIGHT IT WAS.
SOMEONE'S TRYING TO MAKE A POINT. SOMEONE'S TRYING TO ESCALATE THINGS...

... AND HERE WE THOUGHT THE OLD MAN HAD ONE FOOT OUT THE DOOR...!
OBVIOUSLY HE WAS SETTING US UP... LETTING US THINK HE WAS JUST GOING TO ROLL OVER --

-- AND WE JUST GOT BITCH SLAPPED!
WE DON'T HAVE ENOUGH INTEL TO GO ON HERE, BOSS. MAYBE THE OPERATOR CAN FIND OUT --
YOU MIGHT BE RIGHT ABOUT THAT...
... BUT OUR MAN, ALBERT, IS CURRENTLY UNAVAILABLE. WE'VE SENT HIM TO CHASE ANOTHER LEAD, UNRELATED TO THIS SITUATION.
HE'S IN TERYZIKSTAN RIGHT NOW...

‹ UH'M NOOKIN' FUH DUH UNSHENT DEMPUL UH THOOL UND DERE ARKIDES. DEH THED TO FUD YOU -- ›*
‹ I CANNOT UNDERSTAND A THING YOU ARE SAYING. ARE YOU SPEAKING IN TERYZIK? ›
* - TRANSLATED FROM TERYZIK
I'M LOOKING AT THIS AS T LAST GASP OF A DYING REGI HE'S HANGING ON BY HIS FINGERTIPS WITH THIS MOVE!
SO -- WHAT'RE WE DOING ABOUT IT?!
THE POLITICS OF DANCING, EH, CHA CHA...?

THE OLD MAN WANTS TO WAGE A FULL-ON WAR. IT'S OBVIOUS HE WANTS TO GO OUT IN A BLAZE OF GLORY.
AND I'M SURE YOU FEEL WE CAN ACCOMMODATE HIM...
FUCKIN' RIGHT I DO!
THIS IS EXACTLY WHAT WE'VE BEEN WAITING FOR --
CALM DOWN. SOMETHING ABOUT THIS DOESN'T QUITE FIT. IF THE OLD MAN IS RESPONSIBLE...
... THEN HE'S LEARNED SOME NEW TRICKS.
BETCHA THEY'RE SHITTIN' THEMSELVES.
TRUE DAT, REGGIE...
... FEELS GOOD TO BE THE KING, DON'T IT?
WE'RE GONNA DO THE OLD MAN PROUD.
WE'RE GONNA TAKE THIS MOTHERFUCKIN' CITY.

YOU DO REALIZE THIS CITY'S RIGHT ON THE BRINK --

CITY HALL:
-- I MEAN, I CAN'T BE THE ONLY ONE WHO FEELS IT! IT'S JUST NOT POSSIBLE!
YOU'RE THE SATURN POLICE COMMISSIONER BILL... SO I KNO YOU'RE FEELING TOO! THE QUESTI IS -- WHAT'RE YOU YOURS DOING ABOUT IT?!

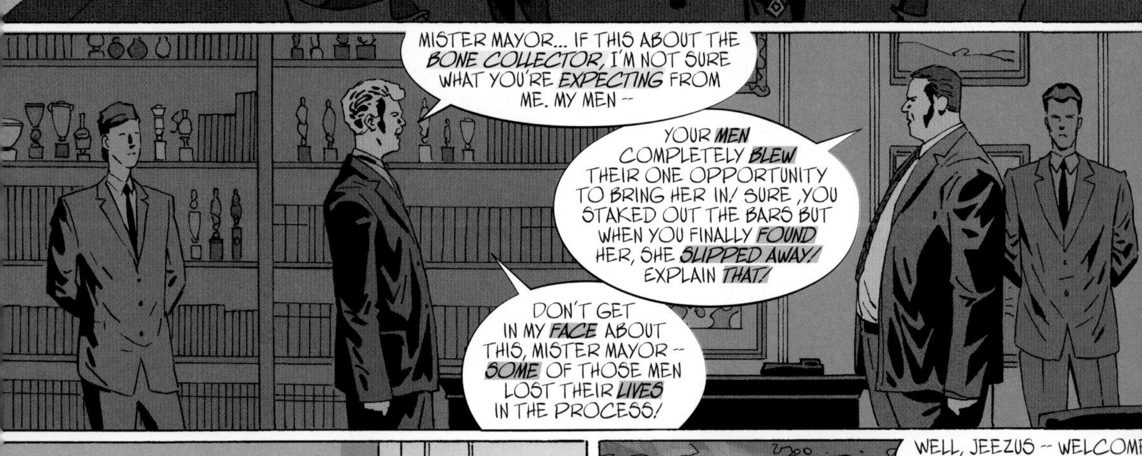
MISTER MAYOR... IF THIS ABOUT THE BONE COLLECTOR, I'M NOT SURE WHAT YOU'RE EXPECTING FROM ME. MY MEN --
YOUR MEN COMPLETELY BLEW THEIR ONE OPPORTUNITY TO BRING HER IN! SURE ,YOU STAKED OUT THE BARS BUT WHEN YOU FINALLY FOUND HER, SHE SLIPPED AWAY! EXPLAIN THAT!
DON'T GET IN MY FACE ABOUT THIS, MISTER MAYOR -- SOME OF THOSE MEN LOST THEIR LIVES IN THE PROCESS!

FURTHER-MORE, I DON'T HAVE ENOUGH BOOTS ON THE GROUND TO ADEQUATELY POLICE THE SHIT THAT'S GOING ON OUT THERE...
... I'VE GOT ORGANIZED CRIME BOSSES FIGHTING IT OUT. I'VE GOT THE TWO LARGEST STREET GANGS GEARING UP FOR WHAT WILL UNDOUBTEDLY BE ANOTHER RACE WAR.

WELL, JEEZUS -- WELCOME SATURN CITY, BILL. YOU WAN TO GET YOU A TISSUE?!
YOU THINK IT'S SOME SECRET THAT SOME OF OUR COPS ARE AS CORRUPT AS THEY COME?!
IS THAT A KIND OF SE TUCKER
NO, YOUR HONOR. IT ISN'T.

IF YOU'RE GGESTING THAT NY OF MY MEN ERE SOMEHOW LUDING TO MAKE RE THE BONE COLLECTOR AVOIDED CAPTURE --
-- I THINK I'M INSULTED.
OH FOR CHRISSAKES. AND THE OSCAR GOES TO...
PARDON ME?!
GODDAMMIT, SEDGWICK --
THIS ISN'T ABOUT ONE SCARY FREAK AND YOU KNOW IT. IT'S ABOUT ALL OF THEM.
THEY SEE THE VACUUM THAT EXISTS NOW AND THEY'RE GOING BALLS DEEP TO TAKE THE REST OF US DOWN! NO MATTER WHAT THE STATE OF THE SCPD --
-- I'M NOT LETTING IT HAPPEN!

ST. MARX HOSPITAL
◄ EMERGENCY
◄ HOSPITAL
◄ VISITOR PARKING
◄ MEDICAL OFFICE TOWERS

SO... FIRST OF ALL, THANKS FOR TALKING TO ME.
HONESTLY, I'M NOT SURE WHAT KIND OF STORY I'M WRITING HERE... BUT, REGARDLESS, I'VE GOT YOU ON DEEP BACKGROUND.
RIGHT...

OKAY, THEN. I'VE TALKED TO THE RECORDS PEOPLE. THERE'S NOTHING ON PAPER THAT CONFIRMS THAT SIMON COOKE WAS EVER A PATIENT HERE.
BUT HE WAS HERE, WASN'T HE...?
WOW. YOU GET RIGHT TO THE POINT, DON'TCHA?
I JUST WANNA MAKE SURE THAT THERE'S NO WAY ANYONE CAN --
LOOK, BENJAMIN...
..."DEEP BACKGROUND" MEANS I DON'T USE YOUR NAME. I HOPE YOU ACTUALLY READ THE SENTINEL. IF YOU HAVE, YOU'D KNOW MY REPUTATION.
I'VE DON JAIL TIME BEC I WOULDN'T UP A SOURC
O-OKAY, I GUESS...
... SO, YEAH, HE WAS HERE. AND, FROM WHAT I SAW, HE WAS SERIOUSLY FUCKED UP.
BROKEN NOSE, BROKEN LIMBS, BROKEN RIBS... YOU NAME IT, HE WAS DEALING WITH IT.
THEY SET HIM UP ON THE HIGH SECURITY FLOOR, SO HE HAD HIS PRIVACY FOR THE COUPLE OF WEEKS HE WAS HERE. BASED ON HIS INJURIES, HE SHOULD'VE BEEN HERE FOR MONTHS.
BUT I HEARD A DOCTOR TALKING ABOUT HOW HE WAS HEALING HIMSELF THROUGH SOME SORT OF EASTERN MEDITATION SHIT...
BUT YOU HAD A MOR PERSONA INTERACTIO DIDN'T YOU...?
WELL, SORT OF... AT ONE POINT, I GOT WORD THAT HE NEEDED A RANDOM ORDERLY TO WHEEL HIM OUT OF HIS ROOM LATE AT NIGHT AND TAKE HIM DOWNSTAIRS.
HE PAID ME. PAID ME WELL. MADE ME DRESS UP LIKE ANOTHER PATIENT -- WHY, I HAVE NO IDEA -- AND HAD ME TAKE HIM DOWN TO THE SUB-BASEMENT.
AS FAR AS I KNOW, NO ONE ELSE WAS DOWN THERE. AND I LEFT HIM THERE FOR AT LEAST A HALF-HOUR.
WHEN I CA BACK FOR HE WAS ST ALONE DO THERE.
LEMME TELL YOU, MISS JEMAS... IT WAS FUCKIN' WEIRD.

WE'VE ALL HEARD THE RUMORS ABOUT SIMON COOKE. RICH AND ECCENTRIC ARE AT THE TOP OF THE LIST, RIGHT...?
BUT I'M ASKING FOR YOUR PERSONAL OPINION HERE. YOU SAY "WEIRD," BUT IN WHAT WAY...?

I DUNNO... THE FACT THAT HE WANTED TO HANG OUT ALONE IN A BASEMENT WAS WEIRD ENOUGH. BUT IT WAS JUST THE WAY HE CARRIED HIMSELF. THE LOOK IN HIS EYES...
HE WAS BEATEN... HIS BODY WAS BEYOND BROKEN...

... BUT HE WASN'T.
Y'KNOW WHAT I MEAN...?
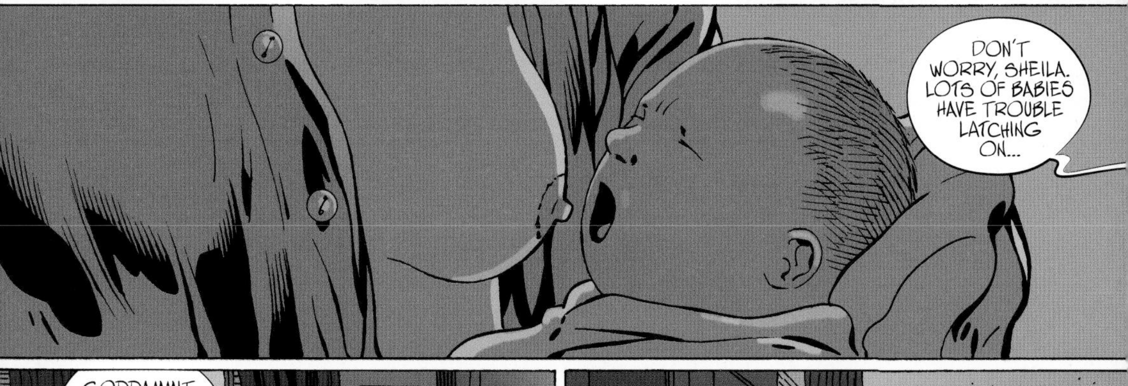
DON'T WORRY, SHEILA. LOTS OF BABIES HAVE TROUBLE LATCHING ON...

GODDAMMIT. THIS ISN'T WORKING...!
HERE. JUST TAKE HIM...
UMMM... OKAY. I THINK MAYBE IF YOU GAVE IT MORE TIME --
FORGET IT! HE CAN HAVE ANOTHER BOTTLE...!

NOTHING LIKE A MOTHER-SON BONDING MOMENT TO MAKE YOU FEEL ALL SQUISHY INSIDE.

THAT WAS SARCASM, BY THE WAY.
SO... HAS IT BEEN THIS ROUGH SINCE YOU GOT HOME FROM THE HOSPITAL?
I DUNNO, MISS LAGRAVENESE...

... I-I JUST... CAN'T EXPLAIN THIS... HOW I'M FEELING...
... THIS BABY... THERE'S JUST NOTHING THERE...

RIGHT.
LOOK, I'M ABOUT AS MATERNAL AS JOAN CRAWFORD. BUT THIS POSTPARTUM DEPRESSION THING...
... IT'S SERIOUS STUFF. I CAN SEE IT ON YOUR FACE, SHEILA.

IF YOU NEED MORE HELP, I CAN PROBABLY --
YOU DON'T UNDERSTAND, OKAY?!
THIS K YOU DO KNOW W IT CA FROM

"IT"? WELL, I THINK I HAVE SOME IDEA...
THAT'S NOT WHAT I MEAN...

... I'M TALKING ABOUT THE FATHER. I TRIED TO BLOCK IT OUT, BUT NOW...
... I DON'T KNOW WHAT TO DO. IT ALL JUST... GOT OUT OF HAND...
F-FRANK WAS Y'KNOW... HAN AROUND THE A LOT. I GO SUCKED IN I GUESS...

... I KNOW YOU WARNED ME NOT TO GET MIXED UP WITH HIM --
WAIT A SEC... "FRANK"--?!
YOU DIDN'T HAVE A KID WITH THE PRANK ADDICT...

... DID YOU...?

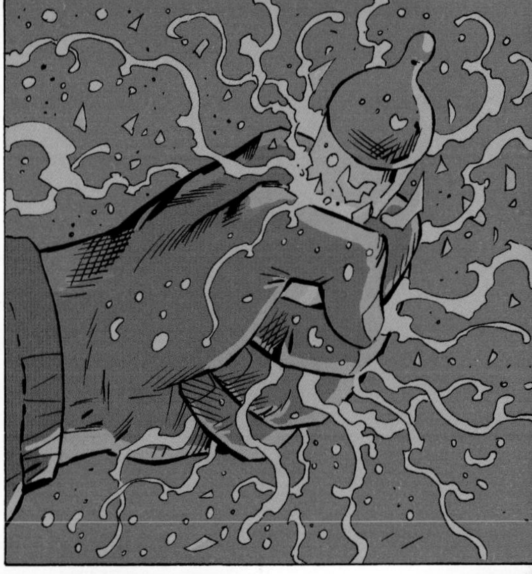

WELCOME BACK TO HELL...

... THIS IS WHERE FINAL JUDGMENT OCCURS...

... THIS IS WHERE WE CAN TRULY LEARN THE EXTENT OF THE DAMAGE THAT HAS BEEN DONE.
I... I C-CAN'T...
... IT'S ALL... OVER NOW...

YOU WERE NEVER QUALIFIED TO JUDGE YOUR CONTINUED USEFULNESS. YOU NEVER KNEW THE ROLE YOU PLAYED.
YOU DON'T... UNDERSTAND. THINGS... HAVE CHANGED... TOO MUCH...
DO NOT SPEAK OF "CHANGE". WE DEAL EXCLUSIVELY IN EVOLUTIONARY CONCEPTS.
OUR MASTER FORGES HISTORY OUT OF THE RAW MATERIALS BROUGHT TO HIM...
... HIS VISION SHALL NOT PERISH WITH YOU.
I DID... EVERYTHING I WAS... SUPPOSED TO DO...
... I-I PRANKED 'EM ALL...
... DROVE EVERYONE... COMPLETELY BATSHIT CRAZY...
NOT EVERYONE.

I-I... COULDN'T HELP THAT... HE WAS... I M-MEAN... HE JUST UP AND --
WE ARE WELL AWARE OF WHAT HAS TRANSPIRED...
... AND YOU WERE BUILT TO ADAPT TO ANY AND ALL EVENTUALITIES. YOU WERE MEANT TO SERVE A SPECIFIC PURPOSE.
MANKIND'S CONSCIOUSNESS WOULD BE FOREVER ALTERED BY YOUR PRESENCE. BOTH OF YOU. BUT THE ABSENCE OF ONE SHOULD NOT AFFECT THE OVERALL OBJECTIVES OF THE OTHER...
... A LESSON YOU WILL LEARN HERE AND NOW.
GYEEAAAAHH--
THIS WORLD IS SO EASILY DISTRACTED. ESPECIALLY BY MEANINGLESS SPECTACLE. THAT IS ONE OF ITS PRIMARY WEAKNESSES.
BUT EXPLOITING SUCH WEAKNESS IS EXACTLY HOW ONE FORGES HISTORY. I HAVE SPENT MORE THAN A MILLENNIA ON SUCH MATTERS. SO FAR, I HAVE BEEN A PATIENT DEITY... A FIGURE OF MERE MYTH...
THE TIME TO ACT IS FINALLY UPON US...

... THE TIME OF VIZ IBN ZIYAD.

I MUST'VE BEEN INSANE TO THINK YOU WERE ANY KIND OF MAN!
WHY DON'T YOU JUST CRAWL AWAY SOMEWHERE AND DIE?!

JUST END IT ALL--!
ELLIOT...
HMMM...?

YOU WITH ME...?
Y-YES. SORRY...
FEELS STRANGE TO BE TALKING TO MISTER COOKE BEFORE I'VE REALLY HAD A CHANCE TO SETTLE BACK IN...

I KNOW, AND I APOLOGIZE. BUT I THOUGHT IT'D BE WORTH IT FOR YOU TWO TO CONNECT... TO AT LEAST GIVE HIM A SENSE THAT YOU'RE BACK AT WORK.
HE TRUSTS YOU, ELLIOT. HE ALWAYS HAS. AND BELIEVE ME WHEN I TELL YOU... WE'RE ABOUT TO ENTER A PHASE WHERE HE'S GOING TO NEED YOU.

WELL, I GUESS I CAN APPRECIATE THAT...
I DON'T WANT TO SPEAK OUT OF TURN, BUT THINGS DID SEEM TO RUN MUCH SMOOTHER WHEN HE WAS A MORE... ABSENTEE CEO.
SPEAKING OF... SHOULDN'T HE BE HERE RIGHT NOW...?

IN THEORY, YES...
... BUT UNFORTUNATELY, ANOTHER MEETING SUDDENLY CAME UP.
ONE THAT HE FELT HE HAD TO TAKE.

THEY SAY AT *ELECTED* EADERS ARE OT *BORN* EADERS.

I SAY LET THEM FEED THEIR EGOS WITH THEIR POPULARITY CONTESTS. THAT'S ALL JUST *SHOW BIZ*, WOULDN'T YOU AGREE...?

I SUPPOSE I WOULDN'T KNOW.

THEN AGAIN, THAT'S SOMETHING THAT SOMEONE IN YOUR POSITION *WOULD* SAY, WOULDN'T *YOU* AGREE...?

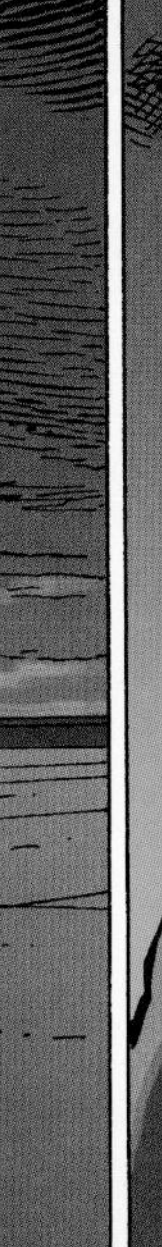

I MIGHT. IF I WAS CERTAIN WHAT THAT POSITION *WAS*.
MISTER WEBER. TAKE A LOOK AROUND. THIS IS *MY* BUILDING. *MY* HELIPAD YOU WERE ALLOWED TO LAND ON.
FOR *BOTH* OUR SAKES, YOU NEED TO BE *BACK* IN THE AIR WITHIN THE NEXT FIVE MINUTES.

AGREED. SO I'LL MAKE THIS QUICK.
I'M ASSUMING THAT YOUR INTEREST HAS BEEN SUFFICIENTLY *PIQUED*. BASED ON OUR *LAST* MEETING --
BASED ON OUR LAST MEETING, I DID MY DUE DILIGENCE.

SO LET'S MOVE PAST THE CRYPTIC.
WHY EXACTLY DOES THE *ROTHCHILD GROUP* WANT *ME*...?

I SEE.
I CAN'T SAY I'M SURPRISED. I FIGURED IT'D JUST BE A MATTER OF TIME. ACTUALLY, I'M RELIEVED.

WELL, IF THERE'S ONE THING I HATE MORE THAN CRYPTIC... IT'S PRETENSE.

THERE'S A REASON WE'VE STAYED IN THE SHADOWS. PEOPLE OF GREAT INFLUENCE KNOW HOW TO PROTECT THEIR MOST VALUABLE COMMODITY.
HOW THEY USE THAT INFLUENCE... THAT'S ANOTHER MATTER ENTIRELY.

FROM THIS HEIGHT... IT'S EASY TO SEE WHAT'S IMPORTANT, ISN'T IT?
NOT EVERYONE IS SO PRIVILEGED TO HAVE ACCESS TO THIS KIND OF VIEW...
... OR POINT OF VIEW, FOR THAT MATTER. IT'S WHAT SETS US APART.

ONLY A SELECT FEW CAN COMPREHEND EXACTLY WHAT NEEDS TO BE DONE TO MOVE THIS WHOLE THING FORWARD.
THE STEERING COMMITTEE THINKS YOU'RE ONE OF THOSE SELECT FEW. THE QUESTION IS...

... DO YOU...?

I LIKE TO THINK I'M UNIQUE IN MY OWN WAY.
BUT YOU'RE RIGHT. MY INTEREST *IS* PIQUED.
SO WHAT'S *NEXT...?*
IT'S SIMPLE, REALLY. WE'LL START MAKING ARRANGEMENTS FOR YOU TO ATTEND THE *MEETING* BEING HELD AT THE INTERALPEN HOTEL TYROL IN AUSTRIA.
BY THE WAY... PRETTY SPEEDY *RECOVERY* YOU'RE MAKING. YOU WERE IN *BAD SHAPE* WHEN I SAW YOU AT THE HOSPITAL.
THAT'S... INTERESTING.
OH, I'M *FULL* OF SURPRISES, MISTER WEBER.
YOU'LL SEE.
YO...
...LET'S TALK ABOUT *YOU* FIRST.
KEENAN WADE.
SOLDIER TO THE MIDDLE. HOT SHIT. HEAVY REP IN RECORD TIME.
BUT WHEN I HAVE AN *INSTINCT*... I *TRUST* IT. SO HERE YOU ARE.
I've done what he asked me to do. I've given him scraps of intel. Whispered rumors about insubordination in the ranks. Nothing too serious.
Enough to justify his suspicions but not enough to get him to chill the fuck out...

... but that's not what this meetings about.
I DON'T WANT US BEING AT CROSS PURPOSES. YOU DIG WHAT I'M SAYIN'...?
AN' I FEEL LIKE WE'VE HAD THIS DISCUSSION ALREADY. BUT MAYBE I WASN'T COMPLETELY CLEAR.
YOU GOT RESPONSIBILITIES HERE. THAT MEANS YOU GOTTA GET YOUR PRIORITIES STRAIGHT.
This is about my loyalties.
This is about Vernita.
SHIT IS ABOUT TO GO DOWN HARD. EVERYTHING WE'VE BEEN WORKIN' TOWARD IS RIGHT IN FRONT OF US.
I NEED YOU DISCIPLINED. I NEED YOU FOCUSED. NOT WONDERING ABOUT SOME BITCH THAT'S GOT YO' DICK WAGGIN' AND YO' MIND ALL FUCKED UP.
The thing is... he's not wrong.
some things get tougher to hide, the stronger they get...
YOU THINK I DON'T HEAR THINGS?
YOU THINK YOU CAN GIVE THIS EVERYTHING YOU GOT WHEN THERE'S AN EMOTIONAL LIABILITY THAT'S GONNA GET IN THE WAY...?!

I'VE SEEN THIS SHIT BEFORE. MANY TIMES, IN FACT.
AND EVERY TIME... IT DIDN'T END WELL FOR THE BROTHER INVOLVED.
I've told her everything. I had to. It's gotten that intense...
nd now it's gotten to the
it where I'm having trouble
npartmentalizing any of it.
WHOEVER SHE
... YOU GOTTA GET
OUR HEAD OUTTA
R PUSSY AND INTO
HE REAL MISSION,
WHERE IT
BELONGS.
ONCE WE'RE RUNNING THIS CITY, YOU'LL HAVE ALL THE PUSSY YOU CAN HANDLE.
THINK ABOUT HOW KINGS LIVE...
... AND WE'RE RIGHT ON THE VERGE OF CLAIMING OUR KINGDOM.
He's definitely been busy while I've been distracted excavating my past. He's turned the Breaks into more than a gang...

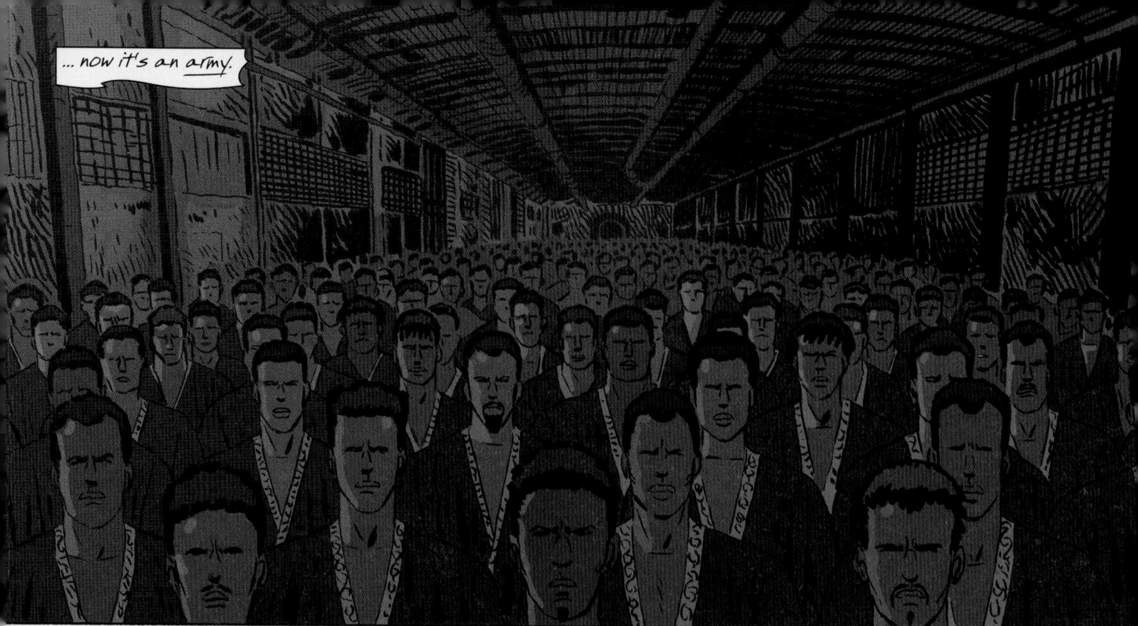
... now it's an army.

THE SKINS ARE ALREADY ON THEIR ASS. BULLCHUCK AIN'T SHIT NOW. WITH THIS KIND OF SOLDIER POWER, WE'LL TAKE 'EM OUT, NO SWEAT.
THEN WE CAN GET ON TO THE REAL OBJECTIVE...

... THAT'S WHY I NEED YOU AT YOUR BEST, Y'DIG?
I NEED EVERYONE -- EVERY LAST BREAK -- AT THEIR TIP-TOP.
I gotta admit, I never saw this coming...

... this thing's getting political.
THIS IS WHAT WE WERE BUILT FOR.
THIS IS DESTINY CALLING.
YOU FEELING ME, BOPPERS?!

-- BREAKS!
DAMN STRAIGHT!

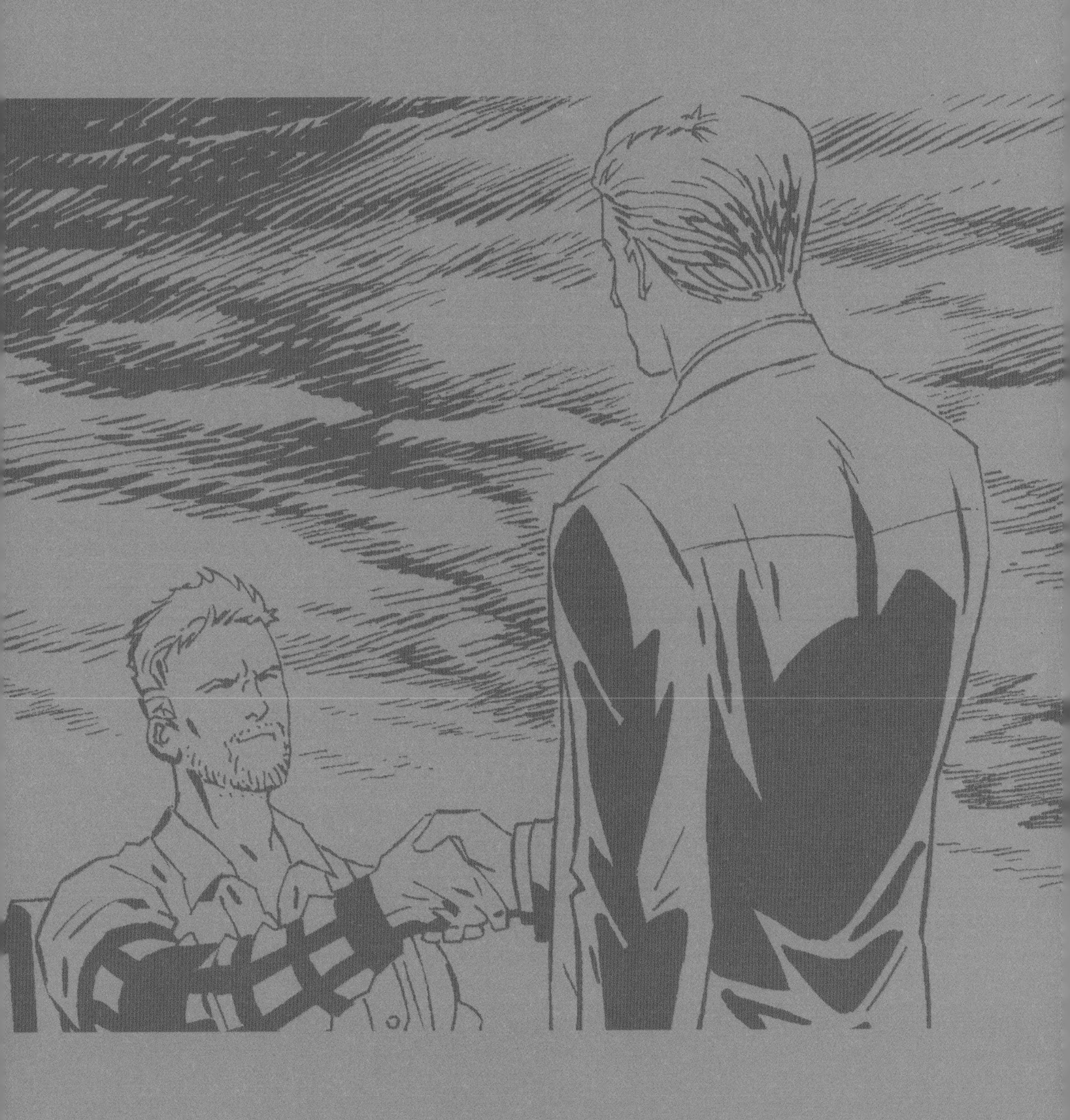

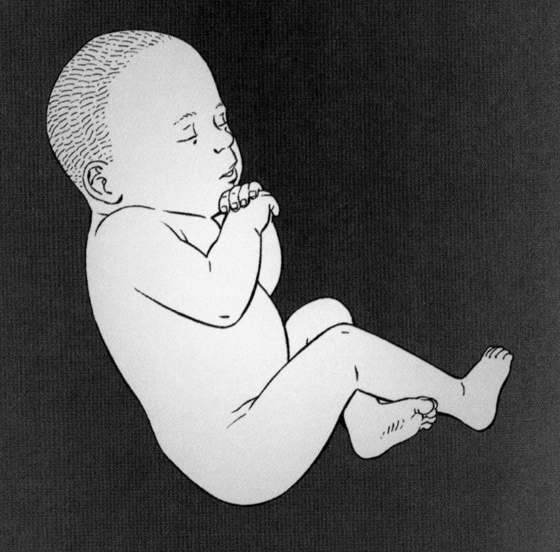

sex

CHAPTER THIRTY-THREE BIBLIOTHÉQUE

JOE CASEY WRITER · PIOTR KOWALSKI ARTIST · BRAD SIMPSON COLORIST · RUS WOOTON LETTERER · SONIA HARRIS GRAPHIC DESIGNER

THE COOKE COMPANY
SO, ELLIOT, YOU'VE BEEN GIVEN PRETTY MUCH ALL THE RELEVANT INTERNAL PAPERWORK PERTAINING TO THE MONTHS YOU MISSED...
SATURN CITY:

... WHAT DO YOU THINK?
QUITE HONESTLY, I THINK I SHOULD'VE NEVER COME BACK.
I MEAN, I THOUGHT MISTER COOKE WAS *FULLY COMMITTED* TO MOVING THIS COMPANY *FORWARD.*

I CAN'T IMAGINE SPIKING THE KANSEI DEAL DOING HIM ANY FAVORS WITH THE *BOARD*, DID IT...?

YEAH, THEY'VE BEEN VACILLATING ON A *NO CONFIDENCE* VOTE.
THEY DON'T HAVE IT IN THEM...

... OTHERWISE THEY WOULD'VE DONE IT *YEARS* AGO.
MISTER COOKE RECRUITED THE BOARD MEMBERS *SPECIFICALLY* SO THEY WOULDN'T EVER *CHALLENGE* HIM.
THAT LEAVES *US*, DOESN'T IT?

I MEAN, IT'S JUST ONE OF *MANY* REASONS WE NEED YOU BACK ON THE CLOCK.
I DON'T WANT THIS COMPANY GOING TO HELL.

I GUESS... I DON'T EITHER.
BUT THE THING IS, LARRY... I JUST DON'T FEEL COMPLETELY CONFIDENT IN MY ABILITY TO BE OF ANY SUBSTANTIVE HELP HERE...
ELLIOT. YOU'RE THE CFO. I'M JUST GLAD WE CAN FINALLY BENCH THE INTERIM GUY. HE WAS A PAIN IN MY ASS.
BUT I CAN SEE YOU'RE... CONFLICTED ABOUT THIS.
WHAT'S GOING ON AT HOME, ELLIOT...?
...
I'D... RATHER NOT TALK ABOUT IT.
NOW THAT'S WHAT I CALL FOCUS...

... SO IS THIS SOME KIND OF EASTERN THING?
SOMETHING LIKE THAT.
HOW'D YOU GET IN HERE WITHOUT ME HEARING YOU?
SAME WAY I ALWAYS DO. ONE OF MY MANY TALENTS.
I'M SURE YOU CAN APPRECIATE THAT.
IF YOU DON'T MIND... YOU CAN SEE I'M IN NO POSITION TO FIND MYSELF ON THE RECEIVING END OF ANY OF THEM.
I CAN SEE THAT.
THERE'S ALWAYS SOMETHING TO BE SAID FOR A QUICK REFRACTORY PERIOD. BUT THAT'S NOT WHY I'M HERE.
I DIDN'T THINK SO.
YOU DID ME A REAL FAVOR HELPING TO SUSS OUT THE ROTHCHILD GROUP'S INTEREST IN ME. I GUESS I OWE YOU.
SO... HAVE YOU COME TO COLLECT?
NO, BUT I AM CURIOUS WHAT YOU'RE GOING TO DO WITH THAT INFORMATION.
YOU KNOW THE "ROTHCHILDREN" ARE A FORCE OF THEIR OWN. THEY OPERATE AT LEVELS SO HIGH ONLY DOGS CAN HEAR.
YEAH, WELL... THE FACT THAT YOU'RE WARNING ME OFF THEM IS AN ENCOURAGING SIGN.
TRUST ME, ANNABELLE, I'VE HEARD IT FROM ALL SIDES. MY OWN ADVISORS CERTAINLY AREN'T THRILLED WITH ME.

IT WAS A LOT SIMPLER ON THE LEVEL WE USED TO OPERATE ON. YOU KNEW EXACTLY WHO YOUR ENEMY WAS.
BUT I'VE BEEN DOING MY RESEARCH ON THESE PEOPLE. THEY WANT TO RUN THE WORLD...
... AND I GUESS THEY THINK I CAN HELP THEM DO IT.
FIRST OF ALL, I'M NOT WARNING YOU OFF ANYTHING.
SECOND OF ALL... THEY MIGHT BE RIGHT.
I MEAN, WHO BETTER TO IMPOSE THEIR W ON AN OBVIOUS BROKEN SYSTEM?
THAT WAS YOUR WHOLE SHTICK, WASN'T IT?
OF COURSE, IT DIDN'T WORK OUT SO WELL FOR YOU THE FIRST TIME. WHY WOULD THIS BE ANY DIFFERENT...?

MAYBE IT'S JUST ANOTHER VERSION OF --
I DON'T KNOW WHAT YOU'RE IMPLYING WITH YOUR LITTLE SPEECH... BUT YOU CAN STOP RIGHT THERE.

WHETHER IT'S A COMPULSION OR NOT, YOU KNOW AS WELL AS I DO THAT THESE PEOPLE ARE DANGEROUS.
THEY OPERATE IN SECRET AND ARE COMPLETELY CONVINCED THAT THEY'RE UNTOUCHABLE.

WE'LL SEE ABOUT THAT.

... SO THE WAY I SEE IT, WE GOT A *FEW* CANDIDATES TO CHOOSE FROM.
WELL, LET'S JUST PLAY IT *SMART*, COMRADES --

-- WE TAKE OUT *ONE* OF THESE HIGH-RANKERS AND WE'RE ON OUR WAY.
SO LET'S TALK ABOUT *WHICH* ONE.
C'MON, DREXLER... DOES IT *MATTER?*
ARE YOU FUCKIN' *SERIOUS?* HELL, *YES,* IT MATTERS.
MASAI'S GOT A STRATEGIC MIND. HE KNOWS HOW TO STAY ON TOP. *THAT* MEANS THE BREAKS ARE LIKE A HOUSE OF CARDS...

... REMOVE THE *RIGHT* CARD, YOU CAN KNOCK THE WHOLE DAMN *THING* DOWN.
SO WHO'S THE LUCKY MOTHERFUCKER, THEN...?
OH, *THIS* PRICK IS LUCKY IN MORE WAYS THAN *ONE*.
OUT OF ALL OF MASAI'S LIEUTENANTS, THIS ONE SHINES THE BRIGHTEST. WE TAKE *HIM* DOWN, WE'LL BE DOIN' SOME *REAL* DAMAGE. SO OUR TARGET'S NAME...
... IS *KEENAN WADE.*

YO, SKYSCRAPER. I DON'T KNOW IF YOU SHOULD BE DOIN' THIS RIGHT NOW...
... Y'KNOW, MASAI SAYS IT'S ALL HANDS ON DECK. YOU BEEN HOLED UP HERE FOR LIKE A WEEK NOW.

I MEAN, WHAT ARE YOU? PERMANENT BABYSITTER?
I DON'T THINK THIS IS THE WAY INTO SHEILA'S HEART --
NOT NOW, K...
NOT NOW...?
THIS IS SERIOUS SHIT, MAN. MASAI'S GONNA BE MAKIN' HIS BIG MOVES AND, I'M TELLIN' YOU, YOU GOTTA BE THERE FOR IT! HE AIN'T GONNA CARRY NO STRAGGLERS, Y'DIG?

OKAY. LEMME PUT THE KID DOWN, WILLYA...?
I DON'T WANNA BE SAYIN' WHAT I WANNA SAY WHILE I'M HOLDING HIM...
SO, SHEILA'S OLD BOSS WAS OVER HERE AN' THEY WERE TALKIN'. I WAS LISTENING.
YOU REMEMBER THE PRANK ADDICT? CRAZY CRIMINAL MOTHERFUCKER...
Y-YEAH... I GUESS I DO...
WELL, I'M GONNA FIND HIM...
... AND I'M GONNA KIL HIM.

WAIT. YOU'RE SAYIN'... HE'S THE FATHER?!
LISTEN, 'SCRAPE. YOU DON'T WANNA BE MESSIN' WITH NO PRANK ADDICT. BELIEVE ME --
YO, MAN...

NO, I'M FUCKIN' SERIOUS AS A HEART ATTACK.
I CAN'T LET YOU LOSE SIGHT OF YOUR PRIORITIES. YOUR COMMITMENT TO THE BREAKS. MASAI AIN'T GONNA STAND FOR IT.

NOW IT'S TIME TO TALK TO SHEILA SO YOU AND I CAN ROLL UP OUTTA HERE...!
AWWW, MAN... SHE DON'T WANNA SEE NOBODY --
OKAY, OKAY...!
SHE CAN'T KEEP AVOIDING HER OWN KID! IT AIN'T HEALTHY...

YO, SHEILA...
... DAMN, GIRL... YOU KEEPIN' IT DARK IN HERE, AIN'T YA?

L-LISTEN... UMMM... YOUR LITTLE BOY OUT THERE...
I THINK... HE REALLY NEEDS HIS MOMMA --

GODDAMN YOU --
-- I DON'T WANNA HEAR ABOUT HIM!
SHEILA --

I DON'T WANNA KNOW ABOUT HIM!
WHOA -- C'MON, DON'T --
GET THE FUCK OOOUUTTT--!

OOOOUUUTT!!
UNNFF--!

SEE? SHE'S OUTTA HER TREE...!
TOLD YOU, MAN...

-- IT'S A GODDAMN MESS DOWN HERE!
I WOULDN'T EVEN CLASSIFY THIS AS A SMASH-N-GRAB --

WHATSAPP CALL
-- THEY JUST TORCHED OUR INVENTORY RIGHT ON THE DOCK!
WE HEAR YOU, GOOSEMAN..

... SOMEONE'S STILL TRYING TO FUCK WITH THE OLD MAN AND HIS BUSINESS.
NO DOUBT ABOUT IT, RAYMOND --
THERE'S NOT MUCH ELSE WE CAN DO HERE... JUST COLLECT THE BODIES AND SCRAM.
-- AND THEY'RE GETTING SLOPPY, TOO. I MEAN, THIS SHIT IS JUST OUT AND OUT APOCALYPTIC. NO FINESSE WHATSOEVER.

DO WHAT YOU CAN NOT TO LEAVE ANY FINGERPRINTS, GOOSEMAN.
OBVIOUSLY, SOMEONE'S GETTIN' FRUSTRATED THAT WE AIN'T JUST LAYIN' DOWN IN FRONT OF 'EM...

WE'VE BEEN TRYING TO FIGURE OUT WHO THE ENEMY IS...
... BUT THIS SHIT'S GONNA KEEP ESCALATING IF WE DON'T --
HOLD ON, BIG MAN.
I'M SEEING SOMETHING HERE.

... I THINK THEY FINALLY SIGNED THEIR NAME.

TERYZIKSTAN; TEMPLE OF ZUUL; THE ARCHIVES:

HAVE LLED A EAT ANCE, EN'T U...?
UH-!
UM THORRY... DUH GUTKEEPUH LUT MUH UHN. UH DUDT NUH UNNYUHN WUZ UN HUH...
I HAVE ALWAYS BEEN HERE.
THE MANY MILES TRAVERSED ARE MERELY ONE DIMENSION. THE DISTANCE BETWEEN THE IDEAS WITHIN YOUR MIND...
... THAT IS A DIMENSION WHICH OCCUPIES A SPAC MUCH HIGHER, WOULDN'T YOU AGREE?
THE GATEKEEPER KNEW WHAT HE WAS DOING.
YUH... UM... UHHH... ULBUTT UHZENHUWUH...
... Y-YUH C UNDUHSTUN MUH?!

INDEED I CAN.
THEN AGAIN, MY POSITION... MY INSIGHT... THEY ARE BORNE OUT OF A UNIQUE PERSPECTIVE. ONLY I KNOW SUCH TERRIBLE TRUTHS.
CAN YOU EVEN ARTICULATE THE REASONS YOU ARE HERE...?
UM... NUT SUH. UH WUZ SUNT HUH BUH... DERRUBUL PUHPUL...
SENT HERE BY TERRIBLE PEOPLE, YOU SAY...
YUTH... BUH UH WUNDED TUH CUM. YUH-SUH UH HUV DUS BUK...

... UND UM FUHLUH CUHTUHN UT CUMS FRUHM DUS PLUZ...
IT CERTAINLY DOES. I RECOGNIZE THIS BOOK.

CERTAIN TOMES HAVE BEEN KNOWN TO ESCAPE INTO THE WILD. I'M SURPRISED THE PAGES HAVEN'T FADED TO BLACK.
YOU ARE A SEEKER, ALBERT EISENHOWER. I CAN SMELL IT ON YOU.
BUT YOU DON'T KNOW WHAT IT IS YOU TRULY SEEK, DO YOU...?
DUHR WUZ UH PURDUCULUH NUHM...
THERE ALWAYS IS.
AND ONLY ONE NAME WOULD BRING YOU ALL THIS WAY... WITH ALL YOUR QUESTIONS.
COME... LET US TRY AND FIND THE ANSWERS TOGETHER.

I'M CERTAIN BY NOW YOU ARE QUESTIONING EVERYTHING AROUND YOU. WHAT IS REAL AND WHAT IS NOT.
WHAT YOU ARE... WHAT YOU HAVE ALWAYS BEEN... IS MERELY A WEAPON.
A WEAPON THAT HAS MALFUNCTIONED. A GUIDED MISSILE THAT SOMEHOW MISSED ITS TARGET. TECHNOLOGY HAS ITS RISKS.
BUT YOU ARE, IN REALITY, ONLY ONE HALF OF A GREATER FAILURE THAT MUST NOW -- FINALLY -- BE ADDRESSED...
... THE WORLD NEEDED THIS DANCE... THIS CHOREOGRAPHED CHAOS...
... IT STILL DOES.
BUT YOU AND YOUR OPPOSITE NUMBER HAVE SOMEHOW BETRAYED YOUR PROGRAMMING. MY GRAND EXPERIMENT IN HUMAN ENGINEERING HAS MORPHED INTO SOMETHING THAT NO LONGER SUITS MY NEEDS.
I MUST TAKE ACTION. AND SO I HAVE.
YOU WERE SUCH A LOST SOUL. I GAVE YOU FOCUS. AND YOU COULD NOT MAINTAIN IT.

... NNNNN...
... HUH...
... HEH... HA...
I'M SURE YOU SEE ALL THIS AS SOME SORT OF ELABORATE PRANK...
HUHHA-HA-HA-HA...
... YOUR PSYCHE WAS CRAFTED SPECIFICALLY -- BY ME -- TO THINK THAT WAY.
BUT LET ME ASSURE YOU, "PRANK ADDICT"...
HAHAHAHA-HYEEAHHH
... YOU ARE BEING BROKEN AND CREATED ALL OVER AGAIN.
SURRENDER TO IT.
ACCEPT THE TRUTH OF YOUR EXISTENCE.
HEHEEHAHAHAH
HAHAHAHA-
HEHAHAHAHAHA
BWHAHAHAHA
HAHAHAHAHAH

THE SENTINEL:
DON'T GIVE ME THAT LOOK, MITCH. I KNOW THAT LOOK.
JUST SAY WHAT YOU'RE THINKING ALREADY...!
I THINK THA YOU AND I BO KNOW THAT T STORY IS GO NOWHERE...
YOU THINK I'M OBSESSED, IS THAT IT? C'MON...
HOW CAN YOU EVEN LOOK AT SIMON COOKE AND THINK THERE'S NOTHING THERE...?!
DID I SAY THAT? I DON'T THINK I SAID THAT, JEMAS.
BUT WHAT I HAVE SAID ALL ALONG... THERE'S A BIG DIFFERENCE BETWEEN BEING ECCENTRIC AND BEING NEWSWORTHY.
YOU KEEP MAKING YOUR CASE. I CAN SEE YOU'RE SERIOUS.
BUT I'M REACHING MY LIMIT.
SO THIS IS HOW THE DAYLIGHT PEOPLE PASS THE TIME...
... VERY INTERESTING. YOU FOLKS PUT ON A CONVINCING SHOW.
C'MON IN. LET'S TALK.

NOW YOU WANT TO TALK...? I SHOW UP AT YOUR PLACE OF BUSINESS AND YOU LEAVE ME STRANDED IN THE MIDDLE OF A VD PICNIC. WISH I COULD RETURN THE FAVOR.
OH, I'LL BET.
STILL CHASING THE BIG STORY, I'M ASSUMING.
GET ANYWHERE WITH ANYONE ELSE YOU'VE TALKED TO?
NO FURTHER THAN I DID WITH YOU, MISS LAGRAVENESE.
PLEASE... CALL ME ANNABELLE.
AREN'T YOU WONDERING WHY I'M SITTING AT YOUR DESK?

DAMN IOUS, AH.
BUT AFTER THE LITTLE ND GAME YOU AYED AT YOUR LUB... I'M MORE THAN A LITTLE SUSPICIOUS.
SO TELL ME.
THIS... SIMON COOKE THING... I CAN UNDERSTAND IF YOU'RE ON SOME SORT OF CONSPIRACY JAG. I MEAN, I WOULDN'T BLAME YOU.
THERE'S SMOKE... AND THEN THERE'S FIRE, RIGHT?
Y'KNOW, I'M NOT ONE FOR GOSSIP. I THINK PEOPLE... SHOULD KEEP THEIR SECRETS.
WHAT I'M SAYING IS, THIS ISN'T EASY FOR ME --
THIS IS SOME PERFORMANCE, ANNABELLE...
... BUT DON'T JERK ME AROUND. I DON'T HAVE TIME FOR IT.

RIGHT.
WELL, IN THAT CASE, I'LL LET YOU GET BACK TO IT. YOU'RE OBVIOUSLY ON THE VERGE OF BREAKING THIS STORY *WIDE OPEN.*

H-HEY, HOLD ON...
LET ME SAVE YOU THE TROUBLE OF HAVING TO TAP INTO YOUR SKILLS AS A REPORTER... YOUR ABILITY TO PUT *TWO* AND *TWO* TOGETHER...
... SOMEONE WAS ON YOUR COMPUTER.
WASN'T ME, THOUGH.

ROTHCHILD RUMOR MILL
MEETING TO TAKE PLACE IN AUSTRIAN ALPS?

ET ME GET
O STRAIGHT:
TELL ME TO
E OVER TO
PLACE, AND
U'RE NOT
EN HERE?
Y'KNOW, I'VE GOT MY OWN APARTMENT TO HANG OUT ALONE IN...
C'MON, VERNITA...

... I'M SORRY, OKAY? I DIDN'T KNOW I'D GET STUCK OVER HERE.
SOME WEIRD SHIT IS GOING DOWN...
KEENAN! IS THAT A BABY I'M HEARING...?!

WELL, HERE'S THE THING --
WHAT THE HELL...?
DON'T DO IT, GIRL!

C'MON BACK T'ME, SHEILA!
PLEASE--!

OH SHIT--!

THIS IS CRAZY, GIRL! THIS AIN'T THE ANSWER TO NOTHIN'!
Y'GOTTA GET DOWN FROM THERE --
WHOA! WHAT'S GOING ON UP HRE?!
JEEZUS CHRIST --

SHEILA, BABY!
ALL THIS JUST AIN'T WORTH IT! WE CAN FIGURE IT OUT!
I'M BEGGIN' YOU--!

NOT... WORTH IT...
NO, I KNOW IT'S NOT...

... IT NEVER WILL BE...
DON'T TALK LIKE THAT, GIRL! IT'S NOT --
THINK OF YOUR KID, SHEILA! HE NEEDS YOU --

SOMEONE SHOULD... DROWN THAT BABY...
I-I... CAN'T...

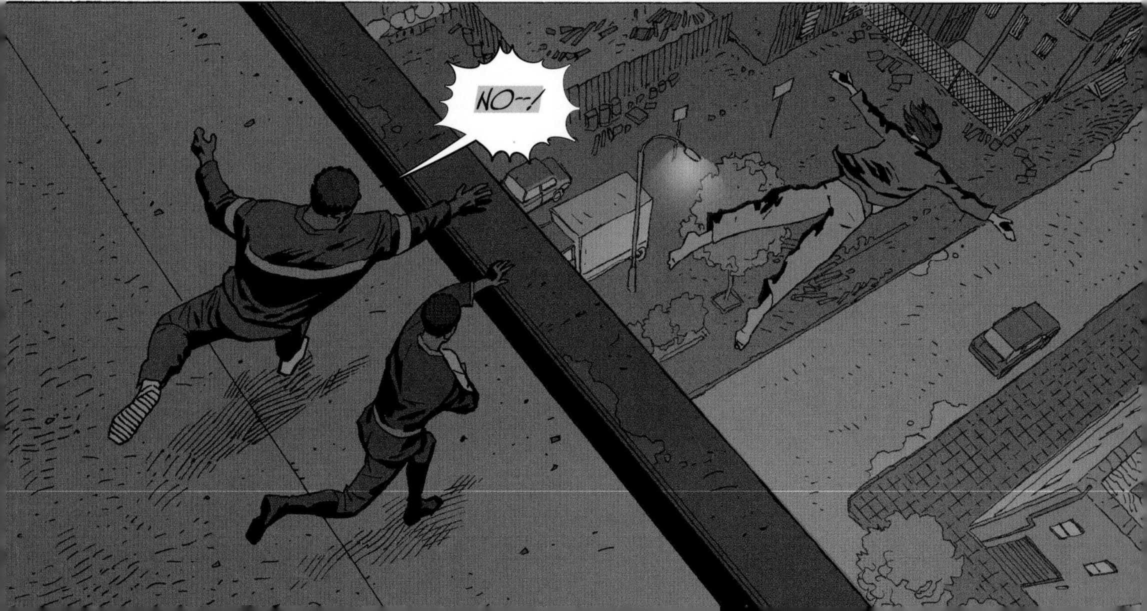
NO--!

SEX

CHAPTER THIRTY-FOUR
THE SHOW MUST GO ON

JOE CASEY WRITER · PIOTR KOWALSKI ARTIST · BRAD SIMPSON COLORIST · RUS WOOTON LETTERER · SONIA HARRIS GRAPHIC DESIGNER

SURE WE CAN HANDLE IT. THERE'S ONLY ONE ISSUE FOR ME...

... WE DON'T RANK OUR EMPLOYEES. NOT THAT WAY. SO FOR THEM TO WANT THE "BEST" WE HAVE IS COMPLETELY SUBJECTIVE.
...
NO, I KNOW EXACTLY WHAT THEY WANT THEM FOR. THE MASTER RACE AT PLAY, RIGHT?

OH, I'M SURE THEY'LL LOVE THE SCENERY --
M-MISS LAGRAVENESE...
HOLD ON...

... IT'S... AAHHH... W-WELL...
... UMMM... WE STILL DON'T KNOW IF SHE FELL... OR IF SHE JUMPED...

... THEY'RE STILL... TRYING TO FIND OUT FOR SURE...
NO...
... SHEILA...

JEEZUS CHRIST...
... THIS CHICK WASN'T MESSING AROUND.
CAN SOMEONE KEEP THE CIVILIANS BACK...?!
AMBULANCE

HEY, YOU...
... LISTEN, I DON'T KNOW IF YOU KNEW HER, BUT WE DON'T NEED ANY TROUBLE HERE.
I MEAN, IF THIS IS GANG-RELATED --
CALM DOWN, SMOKEY...

... YOU GOT NOTHING TO WORRY ABOUT.
THIS IS... I DUNNO... JUST ONE OF THOSE RANDOM TRAGEDIES WHERE THE COLLATERAL DAMAGE IS DROPPED IN THE LAPS OF THE ONES...

... LEFT BEHIND.

GODDAMMIT...!

SKYSCRAPER!
C'MON, MAN -- WHERE ARE YOU?!

DID YOU --

SIGH
SHIT...!

MUTHAFUKKAZ!

THE GODDAMNED ALPHA BROTHERS! THOSE PUNK ASS COCKSUKKAZ ARE THE ONE TRYIN' TO UPEND THE OLD MAN'S EMPIRE?!
WHEN THE FUCK DID THEY GROW THE BALLS, RAY?!

DON'T MATTER NOW, REGGIE... THIS WAR IS ON LIKE KING KONG!
TIME TO SHUT THIS SHIT DOWN!
DAMN STRAIGHT --
NOT TO INTERRUPT THE BROMANCE...
... BUT ISN'T THIS WHAT YOU'VE GOT ME FOR?
AREN'T I SUPPOSED TO BE YOUR WEAPON OF MASS DESTRUCTION?
YOU TWO MIGHT BE ABLE TO RESIST MY CHARMS, BUT THE ALPHA BROTHERS --
LISTEN TO ME, BITCH...
... I AIN'T IN THE MOOD FOR THAT HORNY TONE OF YOURS.
YOU'RE GODDAMN RIGHT THIS IS WHAT WE DRAGGED YOU OFF THE STREETS FOR...!
WELL, THAT'S A I'M SAYIN
WELL, THIS HERE'S WHAT WE'RE SAYIN'...
... NOW THAT WE GOT OURSELVES A TARGET, YOU -- AN' THAT STONE COLD PUSSY A' YOURS -- IS GONNA DO WHAT YOU DO BEST.
MUSIC TO MY EARS, RAYMOND...
... YOU'VE KEPT ME THE BENC FOR WAY T LONG.

THERE ARE MANY SECRETS TO BE FOUND HERE, ALBERT EISENHOWER...
TERYZIKSTAN; TEMPLE OF ZUUL; THE ARCHIVES:

... BUT YOU'VE BROUGHT A FEW WITH YOU, I TAKE IT.
THAT'S GOOD...

... A FREE EXCHANGE OF IDEAS AND INFORMATION.
NOW TAKE THIS...

UHHH... UM NUT RULLUH HUH TUH...
UTH...UTH DUTH DAFE...?

IS ANYTHING COMPLETELY SAFE?
IN THE DARKEST CORNERS OF THE WORLD, THAT WHICH IS DANGEROUS IS AN ACCEPTED COMPONENT OF OUR EXISTENCE.
EVEN NECESSARY.

IF YOU WANT TRUTH, YOU MUST FIRST CONFRONT FEAR.
UHM JUTH HUH... UBUH DUH BUK --
-- UND DUH NUM... VUZ UBN THYAD...

AH, YES... A SINGULAR BEING WHO HAS ACCURATELY BEEN LABELED AS "HISTORY'S HERETIC"...
... A BEING WHO HAS SPENT HIS DAYS MARCHING ACROSS THE UNDERWORLD, LEAVING AN ENDLESS TRAIL OF TEARS IN HIS WAKE.
DUTH UTH... BOWUHFUH THUFF...

INDEED IT IS. AS ARE THE TERRIBLE TRUTHS BEHIND VIZ IBN ZIYAD.
HE IS A CRUEL SHAPER OF DESTINIES. HE EXISTS AT A SUPREME LEVEL...
"... THE ULTIMATE PUPPET MASTER.
"AND YET, HE WOULD LET THE WORLD BURN... AND BEGIN AGAIN.
"ENTROPY AS A CLEANSING AGENT."
UNDRO... PEE...
LUT UT... BUHN...?
OF COURSE, ONE COULD NEVER PRESUME TO KNOW THE MOTIVES OF SUCH A HIGHER BEING.
BUT IT'S GREAT FUN TO SPECULATE, DON YOU AGREE? AND CAN CERTAINLY EXPLORE THE DEMONIC HIERARCHY...
UHHHH...

HE PLE OF IS A ADE...
UHHH... UHHH...
HE REAL OWER LIES THIN THE EART OF S MASTER, A. ITS EVIL LOATS ONG US --

-- NOW LET IT FINALLY REVEAL ITSELF UNTO YOU!

AAAHHH --
--YYEEARRGGH

WELCOME BACK, MAGGOT...

WHETHER YOU REALIZE IT OR NOT -- AND I'M CERTAIN YOU DON'T -- HUMANITY'S COLLECTIVE IDENTITY IS AS MALLEABLE AS YOURS IS.
I LEARNED THIS CENTURIES AGO, AND HAVE BEEN MANIPULATING IT EVER SINCE.

OF MY LATEST MANIPULATIONS, YOU WERE BUT ONE HALF OF THE EQUATION. SO YOU SHALL BE AGAIN.

AND THIS TIME, YOU WILL LEAVE NOTHING TO CHANCE.
YOU WILL USE HIS ATTACHMENT TO THE CITY AGAINST HIM. YOU WILL EXPOSE THE HUMAN HYPOCRISY FOR EXACTLY WHAT IT IS.

YOU WILL SHOW HIM THAT HE CANNOT STRAY FROM THAT WHICH CREATED BOTH HIM...
... AND YOU.

HE HAS DISPLEASED HIS GOD --

-- AND HE WILL PAY THE ULTIMATE PRICE.

... AND YOU COULDN'T FIND HIM *ANYWHERE?* THAT'S *CRAZY...!*
WHERE DO YOU THINK HE *SPLIT* TO?
WHO KNOWS?! I WOULDN'T HAVE THE SLIGHTEST IDEA WHERE TO START *LOOKING,* EITHER. EVEN *WITH* A BABY ON HIS HIP...!
WORST POSSIBLE *TIMING,* TOO...

... SHIT IS *GOING DOWN,* V. *HARD,* IN SOME PLACES.
I WAS HOPING THAT SKY'D BE RIGHT THERE *NEXT* TO ME... SO I COULD KEEP A CLOSE *EYE* ON HIM...!
C'MON, KEENAN... YOU'RE FREAKING ME *OUT* HERE...

WELL, THIS IS SOME *FREAKY SHIT,* BABY...!
MASAI'S TAKING APART THE ENTIRE *NETWORK* PIECE BY PIECE...

"... SENDING SMALL SQUADS OF US
MARCHING INTO THE OUTER BOROU
AND STOMPING EVERY TWO-BIT OUT
INTO *TOMATO PASTE...!*"

WELL, YOU CAN *HANDLE* YOURSELF OUT THERE, RIGHT...?
I MEAN, IS THIS WHAT YOU *SIGNED UP* FOR?

I'M *FINE.* TRUST ME.
BUT MASAI'S LIGHTIN' THE FUSE ON A *POWDER KEG* THAT EXISTS UNDER THIS CITY...
... WHEN THAT SHIT *BLOWS,* IT'S GONNA BE *SERIOUS.*

NOW YOU'RE REALLY SCARIN' ME...!
WHAT DOES HE WANT?
HE WANTS THE REAKS RUNNIN' THE TABLE. HE THINKS E OUTNUMBER THE COPS AND RGANIZED CRIME PUT TOGETHER...

"... AND HE MIGHT BE RIGHT."

WELL... YOU'RE HELPING, AREN'T YOU?!
I GOTTA ASK, KEENAN... HOW FAR ARE YOU GONNA LET THIS THING GO BEFORE YOU STEP UP AND DO SOMETHING?!

THAT'S WHAT I'M TRYIN' TO FIGURE OUT.
ON THE ONE HAND, WE'RE CLEANIN' UP THIS CITY IN A WAY I'VE NEVER SEEN BEFORE.
BUT ON THE OTHER HAND, I DON'T KNOW WHERE THE TIPPING POINT IS...

"... IS IT BEFORE OR AFTER WE'RE TRULY RUNNING THINGS? I MEAN, SOME OF THE NEIGHBORHOODS ARE PRACTICALLY UNDER MARTIAL LAW ALREADY..."

... OUR BRAND OF IT ANYWAY. IN THE MEANTIME --
HOLD UP.
SOMEONE'S TEXTING ME...

?
NO SHIT...!
WHO IS IT? IS IT MASAI...?
WORSE.
THE LAST ASSHOLE I HAVE ANY INTEREST IN TALKING TO...
... WANTS TO MEET UP TO TALK...!

THERE HE IS...

... WALKING RIGHT OUT IN THE OPEN LIKE HE'S KING SHIT OR SOMETHING.
NAH, I'M INTO THIS WADE KID. HE'S GOT A SET OF BALLS ON HIM.
HE IS JUST A KID, ISN'T HE?

CLOSE ENOUGH.
BUT LOOKS TO ME LIKE HE'S ALSO GOT ONE HELLUVA WEAK SPOT SHOWING...

... HOMIE'S GOT HIMSELF A GIRLFRIEND.

I SEE YOU SENT YOUR ASSISTANT HOME FOR THE NIGHT...
... SO WHAT ARE YOU STILL DOING HERE?
RIGHT.
OH... JUST, YOU KNOW, STILL GETTING BACK INTO THE SWING OF THINGS. LOTS TO CATCH UP ON.
SO IT LOOKS LIKE MISTER COOKE IS PLANNING A TRIP OVERSEAS. ALTHOUGH THE PRECISE DESTINATION DOESN'T SHOW UP ON ANY OF THE COMPANY ITINERARIES.
YOU KNOW ANYTHING ABOUT THAT?
I THINK IT'S... A PERSONAL TRIP. GO FIGURE.
ANYWAY, I'M HEADING OUT. JUST WANTED TO SAY GOODNIGHT.
YOU SHOULD GO HOME, ELLIOT. I'M SURE YOU'RE WIFE IS WORRIED...

MEN

... WHAT IS HAPPENING... WHAT IS HAPPENING... WHY-WHY-WHY...
... I-I CAN'T EVEN --
... SO, YEAH, I FIGURED I'D GIVE IT A SHOT...

... I MEAN, THIS PLACE IS LIKE DISNEYLAND WHERE EVERY RIDE IS ABOUT GETTING LAID, RIGHT?
THAT'S WHAT I HEAR. ANYTHING YOU WANT... ANYWAY YOU WANT IT. NOTHING IS OFF LIMITS.

I'VE NEVER REALLY HUNG OUT IN THE FREIHEIT DISTRICT.
I WENT TO THE INDRA ONCE FOR A BACHELOR PARTY...

SOME SERIOUS PEOPLE CAMP OUT THERE. I'M MORE OF A WHITE COLLAR CRIME GUY, MYSELF.
OH, WHATEVER. I'M TALKING ABOUT WHERE TO GET OFF...!
NOT THAT I'M SUCH A PERVERT, BUT IF I WAS...

... THIS PLACE IS EXACTLY WHERE I'D GO TO INDULGE IN MY DARKER IMPULSES.

EMILY CAROL
QUIN

WELL, I'M *HERE...*

... THOUGHT I'D CHANGED MY NUMBER.
YOU HAD. AS THOUGH THAT MAKES ANY DIFFERENCE.

L, *SOME* OF DON'T HAVE ATE-OF-THE- T *THINKING CHINES* TO ELP US DO UR DIRTY WORK.
GUESS YOU HAVEN'T *COMPLETELY* MOTHBALLED THE THIRTEENTH FLOOR...

FIGURED IT WAS BEST TO MEET *HERE.* QUINN WAS JUST ABOUT THE ONLY COMMON GROUND WE *HAD.*
I KNOW HOW YOU *FEEL* ABOUT ME... AND ABOUT WHAT WENT DOWN. AND *HOW* IT WENT DOWN.
BUT I'VE GOT SOME INTEL CONCERNING *YOU* THAT I SIMPLY CAN'T IGNORE...

... RUMOR HAS IT YOU'RE RUNNING WITH *THE BREAKS.*

IS THAT SO...?
I WONDER WHO'S SPREADING THAT PARTICULAR RUMOR...

WHAT'S THE DIFFERENCE IF IT'S TRUE --
Y'KNOW, I'VE NEVER BEEN HERE BEFORE. THERE WAS NO OBITUARY... NO FUNERAL...

... NO NOTHING.
I WOULD'VE PAID MY RESPECTS WH SHE PASSED. B I NEVER GOT T CHANCE...

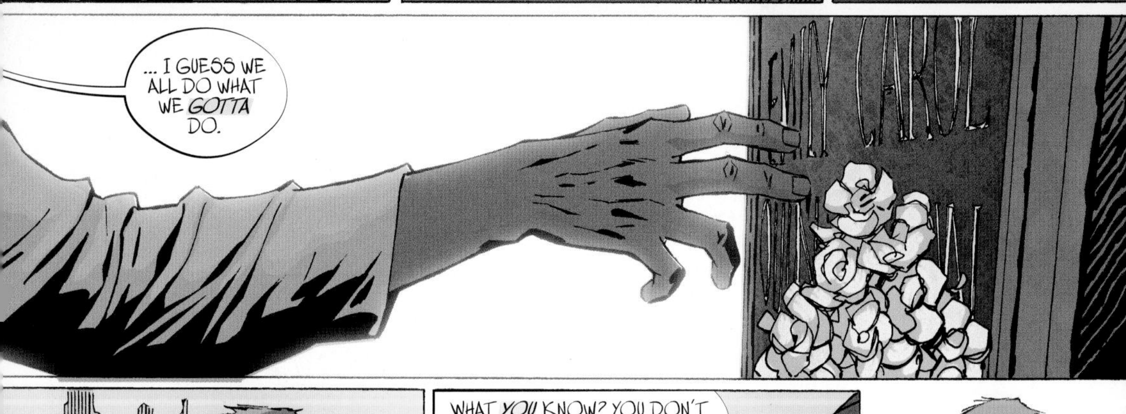
... I GUESS WE ALL DO WHAT WE GOTTA DO.

SAVE THE EULOGY. SHE DOESN'T NEED IT.
AND HOW DO YOU THINK SHE'D FEEL IF SHE KNEW WHAT I KNEW ABOUT YOU?

WHAT YOU KNOW? YOU DON'T KNOW JACK SHIT, SIMON. YOU DON'T KNOW A GODDAMN THING.
SO YOU WANTED ME HERE FOR WHAT -- A LECTURE?
TO USE QUINN AS A WAY TO TRY AND KNOCK ME DOWN?

IF THAT'S WHAT IT TAKES...
EVEN AFTER EVERYTHING THAT HAPPENED, NEITHER SHE NOR I WOULD'VE EVER IMAGINED YOU'D GO DOWN THIS PATH...!
SPEAKIN OF WHICH, AREN'T YO WEARING YO COLORS

AREN'T YOU SUPPOSED TO REPRESENT --
GET THE FUCK OUTTA MY FACE WITH THAT SHIT --

-- I'M EXACTLY WHERE I WAS THE LAST TIME WE HAD THIS CONVERSATION!
JUST BECAUSE YOU PUSSIED OUT ON THIS FIGHT DOESN'T MEAN I HAD TO!

SO WHAT'RE YOU TELLING ME... YOU'VE GONE UNDERCOVER?! THAT THIS IS SOME GRAND SCHEME ON YOUR PART?!
YOU DON'T HAVE WHAT IT TAKES TO PULL THAT OFF. I THOUGHT WE TRAINED YOU BETTER THAN THAT.

IS THAT WHAT YOU THOUGHT?!
SO TELL ME, KEENAN... HOW MANY LINES HAVE YOU CROSSED TO MAINTAIN YOUR COVER?!
HOW MANY SATURN SUALTIES DO U OWE FROM LAYING THIS GAME?!
GAME?!

RIGHT... I DIDN'T THINK YOU HAD ANSWERS TO THOSE QUESTIONS.
WHATEVER, MAN.
SO SAVE YOURSELF A WORLD OF TROUBLE AND GET OUT NOW.
I'M HEADING OUT OF THE COUNTRY FOR A WHILE. I'M NOT SURE... WHEN I'LL BE BACK.

THAT MEANS I'M NOT GOING TO BE AROUND TO SAVE YOU THIS TIME.
SAVE ME...

... HE HAS NO FUCKING CLUE, DOES HE...?
EMILY CARO
QUIN

WHAT'RE YOU MUMBLING ABOUT...?
LEMME TELL YOU SOMETHING, MISTER COOKE COMPANY BIG SHOT...
... YOU'RE NOT AS SMART AS YOU THINK YOU ARE. THERE'S... A LOT MORE TRUTH...

... ABOUT ME AND YOU...
WHAT THE HELL ARE YOU TALKING ABOUT...?!

I'M...
SHIT.

Y'KNOW... THERE'S BIG CHANGES COMING. AND YOU DON'T EVEN SEE IT.
TYPICAL.
HAVE FUN ON WHATEVER LITTLE TRIP YOU'RE TAKING, SIMON...

... IN THE MEANTIME, I'LL BE ON MINE.
RIGHT HERE... WHERE I'M SUPPOSED TO BE.
THINK ABOUT IT.

TO BE CONTINUED

OTHER WORKS BY JOE CASEY

CODEFLESH WITH CHARLIE ADLARD
ROCK BOTTOM WITH CHARLIE ADLARD
KRASH BASTARDS WITH AXEL 13
NIXON'S PALS WITH CHRIS BURNHAM
OFFICER DOWNE WITH CHRIS BURNHAM
CHARLATAN BALL WITH ANDY SURIANO
DOC BIZARRE, M.D. WITH ANDY SURIANO
THE MILKMAN MURDERS WITH STEVE PARKHOUSE
FULL MOON FEVER WITH CALEB GERARD/DAMIAN COUCEIRO
BUTCHER BAKER THE RIGHTEOUS MAKER WITH MIKE HUDDLESTON
THE BOUNCE WITH DAVID MESSINA
GØDLAND WITH TOM SCIOLI
VALHALLA MAD WITH PAUL MAYBURY

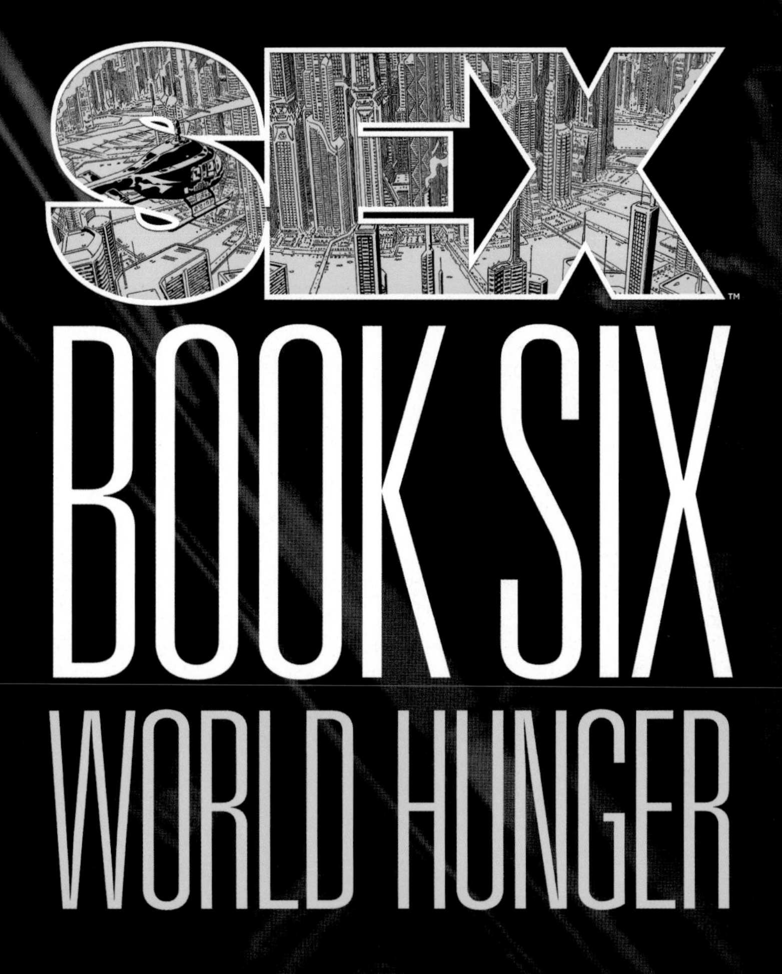

JOE CASEY & PIOTR KOWALSKI

WITH BRAD SIMPSON · RUS WOOTON · SONIA HARRIS

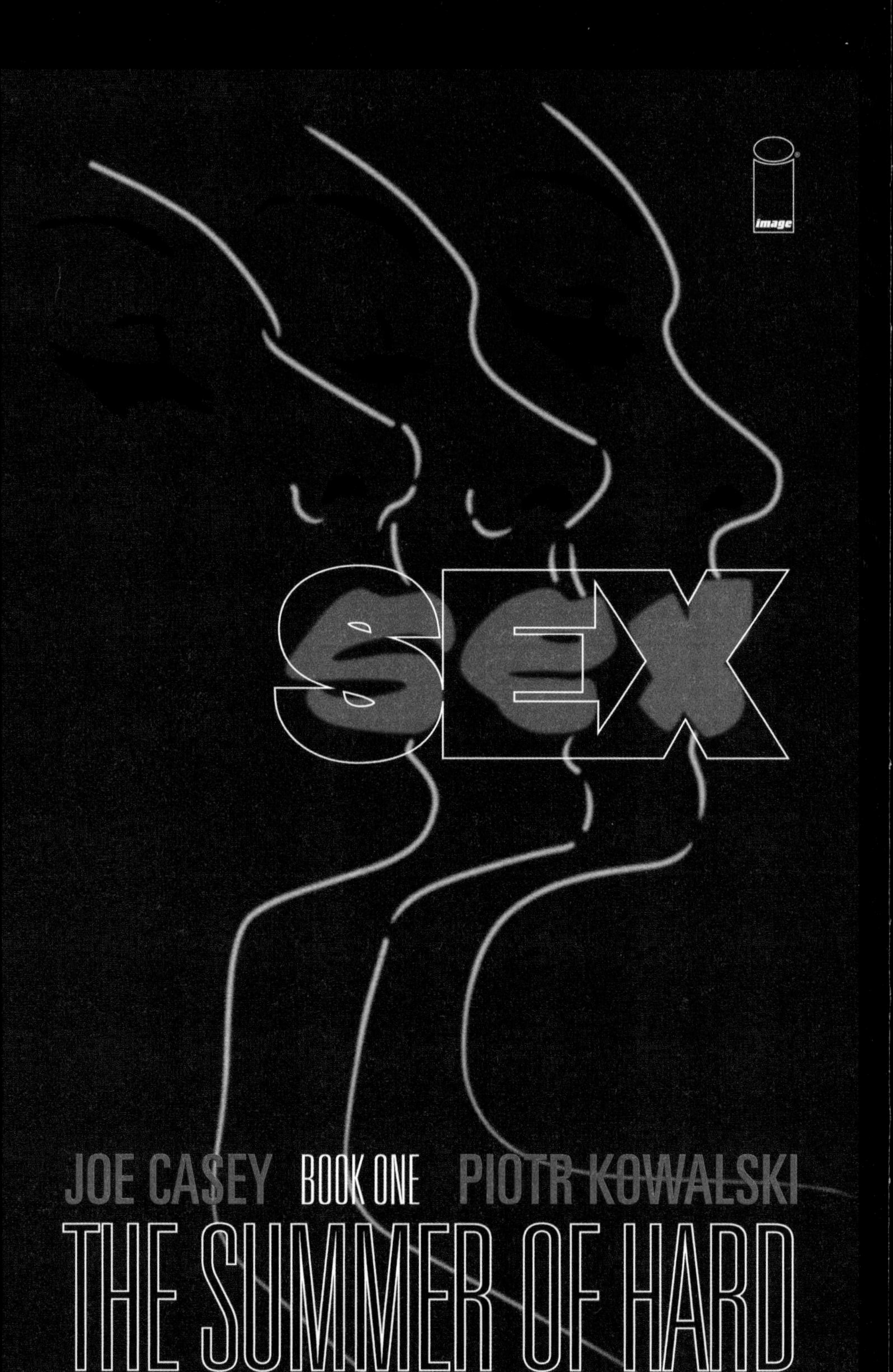
image
SEX
JOE CASEY BOOK ONE PIOTR KOWALSKI
THE SUMMER OF HARD